**A STORY OF ABANDONMENT AND HOPE**

*A Novel*

# OLYMPIC GARDENS

## ANDRENE BONNER

Egwechi Publishing

Published by: Egwechi Publishing, Post Office Box 2009,

Mount Vernon; New York 10551, U.S.A.

Publisher's Disclaimer:
Olympic Gardens is a work of fiction. Names, characters, places, business
establishments, organizations, and incidents are the product of the author's
imagination or are used fictitiously. The author's use of names of actual persons,
places, and characters are incidental to the plot, and are not intended to change
the entirely fictional character of the work.

Bonner, Andrene, 1955-

Olympic Gardens: A Novel/Andrene Bonner/--1st Print

ISBN 13: 978-0-615-26698-5 (paperback)

ISBN 10: 0615266983

Cover Design / Logo by Yolanda D'Oyen

Cover Art by Octavia Ayeisha James

Illustrations by Mabusha Dennis

Author's Photograph by Robert Kazandjian [From Author's Personal Archives]

Interior Layout by Fusion Creative Works, www.fusioncw.com

Printed in the United States of America

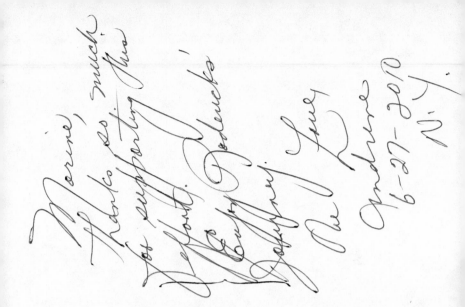

*"I love this cultured hell*
*that tests my youth."*

- Claude McKay (1889 – 1948)
Jamaican and Harlem Renaissance Literati

# About Olympic Gardens

**By the time Roderick Brissett learns** that he is being shipped away from his rural family home to live with his aunt in the city, it is too late. His mother's decision came without questions or answers. Roderick's youth is tested under the most adverse conditions. It is within the abyss of such harsh realities that he must find strength and seek some semblance of joy that will help him to survive, grow, and find his place in the world.

"There is no true word that is
not at the same time a praxis.
Thus, to speak a true word
is to transform the world."

- Paulo Freire, Pedagogy of the Oppressed

# En Memoriam

*My Father*

Egbert Allen Bonner

*1911-1972*

*For:*

All the children marginalized
by circumstances and for whom
education is their access to the world.

# Dedicated To The Generations

*my mother*
*Gwendoline Louise*
*1921 —*

*my daughter*
*Keisha Ruth Melissa*
*1975 —*

*my granddaughter*
*Jamaya Andrene*
*2002 -*

# Acknowledgements

Thanks to everyone who encouraged me to complete *Olympic Gardens*. I owe my highest respect to the complex, yet enchanting culture of my childhood that informed this work of fiction. Some characters, historical figures, and places of historical value are real: Prime Minister Honorable Hugh Lawson Shearer, Walter Rodney, Emperor Haile Selassie, Stokley Carmichael, the Supreme Court, and the General Post Office, and the Congregation of Israelites Synagogue Shaare Shalom. Olympic Gardens exists, however, the enclave that Roderick calls home, is imagined.

Although the Jamaican Movement for the Advancement of Literacy (JAMAL), a national initiative to eradicate illiteracy, was established many years after the period of this book, I am particularly proud to say that I was one of the many teenagers who volunteered to teach in the program. To honor the program, its slogan, *Into The Light* is the title for Chapter 6. Thanks to Shirley Wynter who invited me to co-teach with her, and for such a great opportunity to serve my country.

Adding to the very rich texture of the book are some irie inspirational sounds I love to chant-a-day: *Music Like Dirt* is a celebration of Desmond Dekker's festival song. Phanso and Lij Tafari's reference to *Soon you will find out the man I am supposed to be* is from Toots and the

Maytals' Festival 1966 song *Bam Bam*. *Pantie /fi yuh auntie/Tie head/ fi her dry head!* is a line from a store crier's chant as told to me by my fellow thespian Clive Walker, thanks for the laughs. *While Shepherds Washed Their Socks* is a parody of the popular Christmas carol with a Jamaican flair whose author is unknown.

Sincere gratitude to my darling daughter Keisha who said "mommy I know how much you love Los Angeles but you need to come home to New York and just write", I did just that. To my six year old granddaughter Jamaya who loves books and has been writing her own books, which I hope will be published some day. To my dear mother who listens to me whenever I get excited about an idea and, more especially, for putting up with my papers strewn all over the living room, thank you. To my sister Antonette who read several drafts and made sure that I walked a straight line between the fine cultural nuances of home and creative expression, thank you. To my *little* sister Sandra who can attest to the little child in me who rebels often against injustice, thank you. To my brother Dwight who is one of my biggest fans and who constantly reminds me that our family must always pray together, thank you. To my eldest sister Evadney who can find a laugh in just about anything, thank you. Hearty thanks to my nieces and nephews who are my first audience. A very special thanks to my niece Octavia who used her fictive imagination to capture the essence of my vision for the cover, thank you.

To Yolanda D'Oyen my dear friend who did the cover design and logo for the book and who said, "I am very happy to be a part of this project." Thank you for sharing your insights and sourcing the extraordinary talents of artist, Mabusha Dennis for this book.

There are some very special people who took the time to read a draft, a chapter, or two, at various stages: Dr. Raphael Johnson, Andrea Johnson Orr, Brenda Engler, Angela Bidonne, Janet Henry

Coley, Indira Webb, Rither Alabre, Geoffrey Philp, Sylvia Allen, and Dr. David Conroy, thank you. To my cousin Lorna Owens, Esq., for her unconditional love and critique, thank you. To Jennifer "Sister Fay" Ubiwa who believed that a good laying-on-of-hands releases the creative energies, thank you. To Maxine McDonnough who had the final look at the manuscript.

What would *Olympic Gardens* be without the fond memories of *storytime on the periphery* when I worked at the Jamaica Tourist Board in Los Angeles with Dian Harrison Holland, whose stories of her mother inspired the Miss Millicent character, Paulette "Miss P" Wright, Richard "Dickie" Lue, Roger Dryden, Rosemarie DaCosta, and Donnie Dawson, they all insisted that although I perform my stories, I should publish them.

Above all, to those children and adults on the margins of society and for whom education is their passport to the world; I acknowledge your right to a decent existence. To the teachers who are committed to teach them, and for whom the Confucian maxim—*among the truly educated there is no discrimination* resides at the umbilicus of their educational philosophy, thank you. To Dr. Lynn Quitman-Troyka my most precious Language and Literacy professor, for life, who constantly gives me the writing tools that afford me access to language and the rhetorical art of discourse so that I can continue to develop my writing style, thank you.

To the foundation teachers, some of whom are now only in our memory, who inculcated the value of an education, the importance of observation, and participation in life during my formative years at Central Branch Primary School and Merl Grove High School: Ms. Inez Brown, Ms. Tavares, Ms. Davis, Mrs. Ellorine Walker, Maestro Lloyd Hall, Mrs. Barbara Joanne Martin, Mrs. Gloria Grant, Mrs. Joyce Taylor, and Ms. Yvonne Young. A very special tribute to Mrs.

Edith Rhone, Merl Grove High School's Canteen Supervisor who made sure that my brain was nourished with food whether I could afford it or not. I am sure there are many other shoulders on which I stand and may have forgotten to mention, thank you.

Thanks to my students who appreciate my passion for education, reading and writing in particular. To anyone who would be a friend to someone in need, thank you.

The ink must never dry before I extend a great big 'thank you' to a first class creative team.

# Contents

# From the Author

Olympic Gardens is a story that I have wanted to tell for over forty years. I finally penned the first draft in West Los Angeles in 1998, and often found myself sharing different stages with my colleague Dr. Raphael Johnson. I wanted to write a story about aspects of my Caribbean culture that would be accessible to any reader. It is the story of displacement, literacy, and friendship. I found myself framing the story of Roderick and the family dynamics within a larger social dilemma of the absent parent and interruption of education. Roderick's story is the story of many boys and girls who I grew up with on the island. Unfortunately, those who should care for him had a distorted perception that the brutalizing theory 'Is for your own good' is the catalyst that engenders success. Such dastardly acts of cruelty were merely vestiges retained by a post-slavery society that has forgotten that *the 'fathers' of our flesh chastened us after their own pleasure.*

To add insult to injury, denying a child the fundamental rights to an education as punishment for childish transgressions, and circumstances outside of his or her control, is unacceptable. The agony and humiliation that children faced, was one thing, but the delayed expressions of creativity, upheld by cultural norms, which supported the view that *children should be seen and not heard,* was another.

Children want desperately to be heard, they all learn differently—they all have a story to tell whether they sing it, write it, dance it, draw it, paint it, invent it, or sculpt it—they need these modes of self-expression to be acknowledged. I welcome you to Roderick's world as he takes his journey through the labyrinth of punishment, fear, anger, resentment, friendship, and literacy.

One love…One heart.

*Andrene Bonner*

# Foreword

I met Andrene about 20 years ago, and from Day 1, I knew that there was so much talent bottled up inside of her it needed to be shared with the world. Back then she was living the "Bohemian" life in an apartment on Hoover Street in Los Angeles, California. She danced, sang and acted so well I wondered how such talent had not been snatched up by Hollywood! I was not versed in the Arts by any means, but she routinely bounced her ideas off of me. I felt honored that in between playing Scrabble and discussing the socio-political landscape with her, that my opinions on the Arts mattered. She is one of the main reasons that I write a column today. She believed in me much more than I did in myself.

*Olympic Gardens* is Andrene's attempt to finally share with the rest of the world the stories she's been writing in her head all these years. In today's marketplace commercial success is often used as a barometer for how good one's work is, but a price cannot be put on labors of love such as this. By publishing this work it's already a success in my eyes. Someone once said that "luck is where preparation meets opportunity." If that's true, I know that Andrene has been preparing for years for this opportunity to publish *Olympic Gardens*. I think we, the public, are the lucky ones because we are here to experience the brilliance of such a talented and beautiful person—Andrene Bonner.

**Andrew McIntyre**, Columnist

*The McIntyre Report*

# Chapter One

# Hill and Gully Ride O

Peel Head John Crow was scavenging at low altitude this morning. A slight breeze brought with it the smell of decomposing animals from the gully below. The corner reeked of urine and dog doo doo. The rocky ridge's radical descent into the unpaved roadway left no room for a sidewalk or a place to sit. Roderick's feet hurt. His mother insisted that he stuff his overgrown feet into the crepe, a kind of sneaker, he had outgrown last spring. To avoid the agony from a swift thump to his head, he didn't let her know how much his big toes were screaming for help.

Roderick's mother, Mara'Belle, believed that he was Satan's own self and, over time, she would knock Lucifer out of him. One day she caught him talking to himself. Although, in his defense, he had told her that he was only memorizing timetables for Miss Giventake's arithmetic test, she swore he was talking to some duppy, a ghost from the past.

"The devil is in that boy, no wonder him can't learn," she often grumbled. At the slightest hint of annoyance she would yell, "Roderick Brissett. You mad or something? Boy, if a tump yuh—yuh wet up yuhself!" She meant that he would literally pee in his pants. This was a recurring warning that Roderick feared would happen someday.

When she called him Roderick Brissett, he knew her right hand would come down on his head like a dry coconut, the impact of a ten pound sea stone.

Roderick was no ordinary boy. He enjoyed those things most children would find onerous. He was a very quiet child who preferred to spend his time alone. He often found solace under the safe branches of the tamarind tree behind the outhouse. He was pretty much out of harm's way as long as he did not disturb the wasp nest. Roderick made his own toys from truck tires, bicycle wheels, and old farm equipment from the McGlashan's property. He never played much with the other boys as he was too busy dreaming up his next invention. Nothing pleased him more than when his apparatus worked like magic. For a long time, he was the only child for his mother. When he turned six years old, his mother had a beautiful baby girl, Esther. He never liked playing with her because she seemed so fragile and he was afraid of hurting her. Well his fears won the toss.

The weekend before Esther's fifth birthday, Roderick was pushing his little sister down the hill in his toy truck when, suddenly, there was a loud boo-doom-bum! A wheel had broken, and his truck and baby sister went careening down the hill. Her right arm was visibly broken in two places. She had bruises all over her face. Miss Winnie, a neighbor, saw the whole thing and hollered for help. Roderick tried to mend her before his mother got there with soap suds dripping from her arms. Mara'Belle was furious but drew on every ounce of compassion she had for Esther and kept calm. She held the screaming child who could not be comforted. Mara'Belle took off her apron, made a splint, and wrapped the girl's broken arm, to give it some support. She gently put her daughter on her back and proceeded along the road towards the clinic, two miles away.

"Hush, never mind, I am going to have the doctor fix you up real good you hear," Mara'Belle consoled the child.

About a quarter of a mile along the road, a young man from Content Farms pulled up beside them in his donkey cart and offered to give them a ride. Well, Mara'Belle was skeptical at first, but she accepted the offer in order to facilitate the comfort of her ailing child.

Upon Mara'Belle's return from the clinic, Roderick got a beating so fierce, there was blood everywhere, so much so, that the neighbors cried shame on her actions. Mara'Belle claimed that Roderick was a spiteful child because he did not like playing with his sister. In her mind, there was no possibility of an accident. For every belt lash she lambasted him with her tongue.

"You are as wicked as your father," she charged. "I would rather see you in your grave than send you to school one more day. As a matter of fact, I am sending you to go live with your Aunt Hope. And when she tired a yuh, she can give yuh weh to mi good-for-nothing sister, Lillian. She live free like a bird for she noh have noh pickney fi tie up her foot. You won't cause any more problems for my husband and my family. You will be better off doing bollo wuk."

This was the kind of *goat mouth* that Mara'Belle often wished on the boy, a pessimistic life sentence of servitude.

That night, Roderick's stepfather found him asleep between the tombstones in the small family burial ground near the roadside. People said that his mother took out her rage on the child because she hated swagger-boy Brissett, Roderick's biological father, who had left her at the altar to go and serve in the Navy overseas. Well, that depends on who was telling the story.

Mara'Belle grumbled all night, "You ungrateful little wretch. God know why him shut up some people womb!"

Her rage shuttled between personal hurt and righteous indignation. She packed Roderick's clothes, a bag of red peas, dried yams, cake soap, chew sticks to clean his teeth, a wash rag, and the oldest towel she could find, so thin, there were only a few scrubs left in it. As she paced the house, her husband tried to reason with her amidst the ire. He believed that a little more exposure to Sabbath school would turn the boy around. Yet, her temper was as hot as a coal pot, with burning embers so fierce, iron would melt. Cupidon knew that when Belle, that's what he called her, held on to something, it was no use trying to tell her to let go. She was resolute that Roderick had to leave or she would take her young children away. That was not an option for the goodly deacon. Mara'Belle did not sleep a wink. All night she contemplated, she prayed, she quarreled with everyone, she quarreled with everything, she blamed the recent rains on the annoying mosquitoes buzzing around her ears and feet. Then, she finally allowed herself to settle down to write a letter to her sister Hope in Kingston.

Daybreak was about an hour on the horizon when Mara'Belle stormed into the children's room and dragged Roderick from his sleep.

"Put on yuh clothes. Yuh not sleepin in here one more night." She grabbed him by the sleeves of his night shirt and he fell on to the ground. Sleep in his eyes, he tried to make sense of what was happening to him. He started to shake as if he had a fever. The welts from the beating were raw and tender.

"Lawd God," he prayed inside his heart.

She threw his red, mud-stained crepe at him.

"Put it on!" she demanded.

He tried with his feeble strength, but they did not fit. Mara'Belle rolled her eyes, "Draw on yuh shirt bwoy. Let's go."

Roderick was puzzled; he had no clue as to what had transpired between the beating and nightfall. Mara'Belle told him to pick up his grip, a small suitcase in which she placed his clothes, and then she hauled him down the passage way. Roderick looked back over his sore shoulder and saw his little sister, almost in a silhouette haze, standing in the doorway, wounded. Mara'Belle fired up a bottle torch and the two ventured out into the cold, dark, pre-dawn November air. Roderick did not know what to expect from his mother whose silence kept space between them. He feared that any minute she would explode and beat him again. The boy was in a daze, puzzled, and tired but he had to keep up.

They climbed the fence and crossed over onto the McGlashan's property. They took the shortcut through the banana walk, pass the hog pen and water tank towards the crossroads. The air smelled foul. Out of the darkness, his mother started to grumble and Roderick could see her partially lit face by the flickering light from the bottle torch. "A should a did send you to Lillian long time…she did always a take up for you."

"Lillian," Roderick pondered.

Then Mara'Belle began to hum an eerie tune. Fear enveloped him and he could hear his heart beating in his ears. It was not a familiar tune, it went something like this: *I am delivered; praise the Lawd; I am delivered; what a wonderful freedom; glory, glory, glory.*

"Delivad," Roderick thought. "A what mek she want fe delivad? Lawd. Mi madda tiad a mi fi true." Roderick was overcome with sadness and despair.

Roderick and his mother waited in silence for over an hour on Maas Charlie's piazza. Charlie ran the town square bar and cold supper shop for more than four decades. It was a haven for lonely old men, weary travelers, and boys from nearby Content Farms. His wife, Miss Millicent, sewed uniforms for the children and factory workers in the district. In the evenings, she would fry fish and bammie for her customers. Miss Millicent made the best fried fish and garnished it with pickled onions, carrots, and Scotch Bonnet pepper that made the sinuses tingle. The couple was very fond of Roderick and so Mara'Belle stayed perfectly still so that she would not have to tell them her business. A soft pool of light crawled over the door jamb of the shop; Charlie was up early to meet *first bus*.

Roderick had often gone to the cross roads to meet Mister Gilford's country bus coming in from Montego Bay. Gilford brought the best yellow yams to sell in the market. He would set aside the driest for Roderick's mother. She was his favorite second cousin. Today, Roderick was not fetching yams, he was being sent away like *puss pickney*, an unwanted child from her human litter, to live with his Aunt Hope and her sons whom he had never met. Soon the bus pulled in off the dirt road to a screeching halt. It took a little time to settle because of the uneven distribution of weight inside and outside. It was rusty by virtue of its age and many a muddy road on which it traveled. *Sufferers Luxury Line* was painted in bright yellow against a red and black background. Gilford affectionately called the bus Miss Sull, for short. Never mind that the bus was as old as Methuselah. On the top was a crate that was supported by sash cords, old fabric, and chicken wire. It was filled with wicker baskets, old blanket bundles, crocus bags, and antiquated traveling cases tied with sisal strings and worn leather belts. There were loads of bags that were stuffed taut with food, clothes, and sickness-and-money-bush. Chickens flapped around inside makeshift coops desperate for some air through not so generous apertures.

The sideman swung his wide gait out the door as if he was doing the latest Ska, the post-independence dance music enjoyed by both the young and old. He announced in his country falsetto, "Lumsden!

Anybody for Lumsden. Moneague...next stop!" He was a tall dark man with sparsely distributed white, uneven teeth against ruby red gums. He had red, fiery eyes and the most infectious laughter; perfect for the long journey from St. James to Kingston. The sweat ran down his thick arms, festooned with tightly wound, wooly black hair. He wore a white merino soaked through with sweat and you could smell his armpits a mile away.

"Hello Miss Mara'Belle. Fancy seeing you with your son this morning."

"Hello Phanso," she replied without the slightest hint of fondness. "Tell Gilford a say mawnin."

Miss Mara'Belle was not the most pleasant person in the district but she would sometimes oblige him with a half-smile.

Mara'Belle was the middle child of seven Flowers girls, who felt like she carried the weight of her older siblings, and was often dragged through the mud by the younger. Yet, all she ever wanted to do as a girl was to sing and dance like Ginger Rogers. In those days, the mento band was getting more work on the west coast with the boom in the tourist trade. So, Mara'Belle and her big sister Lillian followed the band to Montego Bay. They sang and danced their way into the hearts of the tourists. In no time, Mara'Belle sought companionship with John Bunyan Brissett, a fast talking island-hopper from Rhode Island in the United States. She was crazy about John, and Roderick was born to them that first summer of adoring love. For a while, it seemed that all was sweet and dandy with the young lovers, but something changed. Mara'Belle said nothing to her sister.

Soon after, the *sister act* ended abruptly when she had a falling out with Lillian with whom she often argued over her parenting skills. Lillian couldn't understand why all of a sudden Mara'Belle was so insensitive to the child. "If you don't want di pickney, give it way but noh treat him soh," Lillian often chided. The last time they fussed over Roderick, they almost came to blows. Lillian knew it was her cue to go back home to Kingston and take care of their mother.

Some years later, as Roderick was just beginning to read, a pastime he enjoyed with his dad, John told Mara'Belle that he had to return to America to serve his country in the Vietnam War. News spread in the district that John went back to America to join his wife and children. This broke Mara'Belle's heart. Saddened, embarrassed, and abandoned to fend for herself and baby boy, she left the mento group and went to live on Paradise Estate in St Ann.

Three months after she arrived in Paradise, Mara'Belle found solace in the teachings of the local Seventh Day Baptist Church. She wasted no time in aligning herself and baby boy with Jabez Cupidon, a deacon at the church, who also served as the postmaster for the district. Jabez was a handsome, kind, and loving man who was highly respected in the area. They were married in no time. A year later, Esther was born and Shadrach the following year. Mara'Belle was very proud of her two new children but often found herself at variance with Roderick. Mazie Woodpecker, the village mouthpiece, who claimed to have a relative in every hotel from Kingston to Montego Bay, was convinced that Mara'Belle was no lady fit for Deacon Cupidon. "Him is a decent praying soul—a respectable and loving man," she had often said. Woodpecker was sure that Mara'Belle was a sour puss, posing like some dry land tourist, a pretentious hussy. Her speakie-spokie round-mouthism was a dead giveaway that she never took a boat around Kingston Harbour, let alone, travel abroad. "This woman ride inna Paradise pan her white horse like a real old Annie Palmer, treating her firstborn like a slave." Woodpecker suspected that the white man Mara'Belle claimed was the child's father, had left her stranded at the altar for a better life with his family in America. Mara'Belle never spoke of her past to anyone. "Hell have no fury like a woman scorned," Woodpecker would groan from way down in the bottom of her belly every time Mara'Belle beat the boy.

The sun was high in the sky as floating, cumulus clouds, like soft Indian cotton, kissed the horizon. Roderick was taking his first ever long ride on a country bus. His mother gave him his grip and handed him over to Phanso. She gave Phanso a stuffed envelope, reinforced with a piece of string that made the sign of a cross. It sent a clear warning that nobody should tamper with its contents or *crosses*—something bad would haunt them for the rest of their lives. She asked Phanso to deliver Roderick and the envelope to one Hope Flowers in Kingston. Although Roderick did not want to leave his family, his feet hurt so badly he could hardly wait to get a seat on the bus.

Phanso made sure that Roderick got a seat just behind the door by a window. This way, he could keep an eye on him. Then he slapped the side of the bus three times to alert the bus driver that all was well.

"Gwaan up driver!" Miss Sull pulled off the curb and headed for Kingston. Roderick looked out the window and he could see his mother waving so vigorously he thought her arm would fall off. She mouthed to him, "Behave yuhself."

He mouthed back to her, "Yes mama," and he felt the tears welling up at the back of his eyes and a knot forming in the pit of his stomach. The operation happened so fast that he never had a chance to say goodbye to his sister and brother. He was used to his mother's bad mouthing with threats to get rid of him but he had never dreamt that this day would really come. Roderick speculated, "What mek her decide fi sen mi weh this time? After mi noh know weh mi a go! Mi noh know town...mi noh know nobody dere." He squirmed in his seat as if to situate the thought in its perspective. "Mi know seh mama wicked but dis time she wicked, wicked bad."

As the bus meandered through narrow dirt roads and half-paved main arteries, Roderick couldn't help but wonder what his life would be like in a big city like Kingston. Nothing had prepared him for this journey; nothing had prepared him for this day. He had never been to a big city before. Up the hill and down the rugged terrain—the bus swerved past stray animals and fowl. All the while, the driver was trying to keep the bus on the road and passengers inside. The green pastures lay idle ahead for miles. A feeling of loneliness engulfed him, and he was disconnected within his silence, on a bus filled with people from all walks of life.

The boy marveled at the magnitude of his sufferings as he gingerly touched a welt that coiled like a spider along his forearm. "Sssssss," he hissed at the discomfort. Clearly his heart was broken, yet he toyed with the idea that perhaps going to be with his aunt meant no more beatings. A small boy, two rows in front of him, knelt on a seat and faced Roderick. He stretched, yawned, smiled, and stared deep into Roderick's eyes. "Mek him a grin soh...look like beatin noh reach him yet," Roderick whimpered. Every muscle in Roderick's face hurt, they had forgotten how to smile. Moments later, the small boy rested his head on the back of the seat and fell asleep. The woman next to the boy took him gently from his kneeling position and cradled him in her arms. Roderick imagined himself falling asleep, after such a turbulent night, in the arms of someone who cared about him as much as his Aunt Lillian, of whom his mother spoke.

The smell of lush vegetation competed with the smell of animal dung that permeated the air in ninety-degree weather. Sometimes the bus got so close to the curb that huge tree branches and lots of foliage would rip against the windows for long distances, sometimes falling into the passengers' laps. Long-beaked white egrets manicured grazing cows in wide open fields that looked a lot like the Serengeti plains.

Cane fields in their perennial majesty told the stories of African slaves whose hands bled from harvesting razor-sharp blades of grass, and whose indomitable spirits still lived at the roots. Rocksteady music vibrated through the bus as the driver danced around corners to the hypnotic beat: *Soon you will find out the man I'm supposed to be—what a bam-bam!*

"Toots and the Maytals at the control this mawnin people! You noh know dem music yah. You a young bud," Phanso said playfully to Roderick. Some passengers swayed to the music while others slept with wide-opened mouths; the fruit flies' hopscotch paradise. Old folks held on to their stomachs and their hats as Gilford sped around narrow corners and climbed steep hills.

"Corner parson!" one daring, wide-eyed, meager woman shouted as she grinned and winked at Roderick. Her dark skin was oily and she smelled of roasted garlic and onions. She could hardly contain the chicken feet she was shoving into her mouth. Roderick knew why he did not like chicken feet; it was those crinkly little toes.

This whole scene took him back to that fateful Sunday morning when he had to chase his favorite red hen around the yard to be sacrificed for Sunday dinner. After he caught the hen, his mother tied one foot to the post of the coop. "Poor Stumpy...Stumpy couldn move...foot tie up tight, tight, tight, pan the coob," he thought. The hen resisted confinement with every breath in its being. She flapped vigorously to escape, but the foot was so firmly anchored. When it was time to kill the hen, his mother discovered that the fowl had a pip on its tongue, a disease that formed a crusty, mucus mass, rendering it unhealthy for human consumption. His mother gently removed the crust and applied some healing oil. Then, she set the hen free. Alas, the foot that was bound was broken. From that day onward, Roderick called the hen Stumpy because she had one good foot and hopped on the stump. "Poor Stumpy."

The bus pulled into the Moneague crossing and a mob of vendors rushed to the side of the bus. Phanso yelled, "Gi di people dem a chance fi come offa di bus noh! Di res a oonu, line up man," he demanded as he tried to keep an air of order for the passengers who needed to get off in a hurry. Other vendors managed to get on the bus to make a quick sale or two, while others ran alongside the bus pushing their wares through the window, shouting:

"Dutchess comb!

"Snow cone!"

"Grater cake!"

"Hairnet!"

"Bad belly bush and Doctor Da Costa rub-up!"

Many folks needed to catch another bus or a private car waiting to take them into the interior. Studious ladies and gentlemen, heavy laden with books and grips, greeted each other with great laughter as they made their way to the teachers' college. Phanso bought Roderick a *back and front* shaved-ice snow cone with ice cream topping and gave it to him, "likkle bwoy, cool off yuhself, is a likkle while before we ketch a Town."

Roderick replied wide-eyed and slightly puzzled, "Thank you sir… but is Kingston me Aunt Hope live…not town."

Phanso smiled, "Is so everybody call the city mi son. Dem call it Town. No problem, is Kingston me gwine drop you off. Just *simmer down…control yuh temper*, the mighty Wailers 1964. Young boy, yuh a baby dem time deh." Roderick breathed a sigh of relief and proceeded to cool off with his back and front. Sufferer's Luxury Line, before long, was bound for Kingston.

Gray clouds crawled at a snail's pace over the sun making the road overcast for a few miles. A slight drizzle affectionately stroked the parched earth, and the smell of newly-soaked terrain imbued the air with a refreshing aroma. The trade winds blew graciously across the bus window and Roderick found himself immersed into a terrifying state of introspection. Surrounded by strangers on a "bus ride to hell," Roderick was feeling alone in a world without end. He felt as if the vibrations from the old bus engine had penetrated his chest making his heartbeat deafening. He fought the sleep with every breath in his body.

Roderick remembered those times when he had trouble sleeping and his mother would read his favorite bible passages to him until he fell asleep. He was bereft. Now, every pothole jolted him into the reality that he was on a journey, an end he could not control. The ride was long and the day felt like a brick oven, heated seventy times seven. Roderick refused to sleep; not only was he curious, he was petrified. He looked out at the landscape, splintered with small houses where children played with dogs, young girls shelled peas, stripped corn, grated cassava, and fanned the flames under Dutch-pots of piping stew.

The river slithered like a venomous snake, playing hide-and-seek between the incandescent tropical water lilies. Somehow, the verdant beauty of some small towns along the journey made him dream of pleasant things. Yet, such thoughts had no place with the ugly realities of life he had to endure with his mother Mara'Belle. This made him hope for a better life in Kingston.

"A wonder what town gwine be like? A wonder if it betta than country? A wonder if it have a big, bright, blue sea? A wonder if it have a river full a fish? A wonder if it cool when night come? A wonder if the children dem get beaten like me? A wonder…a wonder what gwine happen to me?"

Then he became sad again, tired, and sleepy as the disappearing countryside dueled with the uncertainty of city life. Roderick flung his head back against his seat, closed his eyes, and took in the darkness and the fading silhouette of human form and shapes. He folded his hands across his chest as if to protect his heart. Sull went flying through the sky in his dreams, and he could hear his mother calling, "Roderick, Roderick Brissett!" But Roderick did not answer; he was too enamored by the floating clouds that formed like Cherubims coming to meet him at the terminus. Once more, the bus hit a massive pothole and Roderick went in and out of sleep. This time, the frame changed and he was falling into a dark sinkhole inside a river cave. Visions of frightening mammals he had never seen before, janga crayfish, rat bats, hissing giant cockroaches, and all manner of insects. It was hot and the musty walls of the cave seemed to be closing in on him as he slipped and slid in murky waters. He kept reaching for something to hold on to when suddenly he jumped out of his sleep. Phanso was holding his right hand. "Wake up son…yuh reach."

# Chapter Two

## No Problem Man

Olympic Way was the widest street Roderick had ever seen. It stretched for miles north with lots of houses and small establishments lining both sides of the road. Each home had its unique charm—built on the influences of Spanish and English-style architecture and suited to the taste of the owners. Most families owned their homes or rented from an absentee landlord. Aunt Hope's property stood on one acre of land and was situated on the east side of the road, nestled between the Goodmans on her immediate left and the Petgraves on the right. Her backyard was separated from the old Mason by a barbed wire fence. Directly across the street from the shop was the Bliss family whose neighbors on the right ran a small chicken farm and bird food shop, and to their left was an empty piece of land—a dust bowl. The Madden's colonial style house adjoined the open land and boasted a strong sense of affluence. Each home was surrounded by a lot of yard space which made the homes seem far apart.

Hope had converted the front of her house into a small grocery shop and painted its patchy cement façade in brown and beige. A small piazza wrapped around the right side of the house that was once an old porch, which served as telescope, to bring the neighborhood close for scrutiny. A large wooden gate, sprawled between the shop and Mr.

Goodman's wall, functioned as the main entrance to the house by way of the kitchen area. The windows were large four-paned glass with strips of wood frame and a sturdy, wooden, double-door opened on to the piazza. Indoors, there were two bedrooms, a small living room that was once a main dining room. The dark living room was separated from the shop by a mahogany door, and Ms. Hope's bedroom opened into it. A long hallway separated her section of the house from her children's room, which stood next to the only bathroom that served the entire household. At the end of the hallway was a storage room. The kitchen was off the side of the shop with a tarpaulin covered roof overlooking the Goodmans front yard. A long gutter extended from the spiky raised zinc roof where it emptied rain water in a large oil drum—great for dry season. The backyard had lots of trees, a large two-storey chicken coop, an outhouse, and a long clothes line that stretched from the Goodmans fence to the Petgraves. This was the enclave of Olympic Gardens that Roderick now called home.

The first day Aunt Hope brought Roderick home, he felt kind warmth coming from her. She held his hand and led him along the path to the house. She pointed out the way the neighbors kept their yard clean. The Petgrave's vegetable garden was very fertile and green.

"This is how I expect you will keep where you live, Roderick."

"Yes, maam. A so me keep my madda yard clean."

Then his eyes locked with a little girl next door as she watered her garden. He slowed and Aunt Hope, sensing his curiosity, pulled him along. The girl was short and plump with big bulging eyes, thick long eyelashes and bowlegs. To the boy, she looked about his age. She lived in a small white cottage with a low concrete fence with hibiscus hedges and a green wooden gate. His auntie gave him the grand tour of the shop, placing much emphasis on the area behind the counter that would be his position of duty for a very long time. He was overwhelmed by the experience and wondered what was easier; "school in the country with family or this damp, smelly shop."

Then there was a loud noise coming from the rear of the house. In scampered two rowdy boys into the shop. They were his two cousins. He had heard about them but had never met them before. They were Stephen, the older, and Nelton. Stephen was cordial and said hello but Nelton giggled a lot. Roderick felt really weird at first but tried to compose himself as soon as Miss Hope sent the boys back inside.

The patrons were coming in and out by the minute. Hope ran a thriving business. It flashed across Roderick's mind that, "with two big bwoy, why she need more help?" but he shook the thought out of his head because there was no answer. Roderick soon realized that he would be a vital part of this business although he had absolutely no experience on that side of the counter. The customers seemed curious to find out who was this small boy poised to serve them. They hurled lots of questions at him and welcomed him to the neighborhood. Children stopped by to stare and old people simply said their, "howdy-dos."

Around half-past ten, an old Indian man sauntered into the shop. He was very slender with sunken cheeks and gray hair along his temples. The man looked as if he had not eaten for days. His eyes were hollow into his skull.

"Sell me a bottle a Bay Rum son."

"He must be really sick," Roderick thought to himself as he climbed up on a stool to reach the shelf where the Bay Rum shared a small space with the Ferrol elixir and Buckley's cough mixture.

"Here you go, sir. That will be one shilling and sixpence."

The old man shuffled through his pants pocket and came up with the exact change. He held the money tightly between his long bony fingers, teasing Roderick with it.

"You new around here?"

"Yes sir," he replied.

"I have been living around here a long time and is the first I seeing you. Where you from?"

"I am from St. Ann, in the country parts."

"So, where you mother?"

"She in the country."

"Why you not in school today?"

"I have to work in the shop for my Aunt Hope."

"Ah see. Hope is your aunt. I know her from she was a girl, you know. Long before she have them boys. Ever since I came to live in Jamaica, I have been patronizing her mother at the Three Miles roundabout. Mother Flowers has been a good woman. She raised them seven girls all by herself after the old man died in the big train crash." The old man continued as he counted the fingers on each hand, "Lillian, the eldest, Hope, follow her, then Clofield, Mara'Belle, Princess, Sarah, and the little dry foot one, Flora. I gave her that name because when she born she look like a real flowers. I know all them girls names. But my favorite is Lillian. She a very kind, nice lady. Came back to take care of their sick mother. So which one is your mother?"

"Miss Mara is my madda."

"Mara'Belleeeee," the old man said with a flourish. "The long-foot one. I remember her. She ran away with the mento band to Montego Bay. She could sing real good. A real belle she was. I remember her–

"I never know my madda could sing!" Roderick interrupted.

"Yes son. She used to sing with them boys in the band at the Myrtle Bank Hotel. You never born yet. When them sailor boys come back from sea, Mother Flowers would keep dance party at the roundabout every New Years Eve, and your mother would sing and dance in the bar. That girl could hum like a doctor bird. She was a happy child!"

Roderick was puzzled by this storyteller who seemed to know

so much about a mother he never knew. He could not imagine in his wildest dreams that his mother ever had a moment of joy in her life—she was always so unkind to him.

"Why you look so troubled son?"

"Nothing sir."

The old man smiled almost in a mischievous tone, "You look like a good boy."

"Yes sir," he said with a smile.

"I can't promise you it will be easy around these parts. I can tell you though, prayer. Plenty prayers! Hard work. Hard work! And don't forget to be generous! Only way I know will buy your freedom."

"Freedom. Is what that?" Roderick asked himself.

Just then, Miss Hope stormed into the shop. She was clearly annoyed and knitted her brow that seemed to stretch her v-shaped mound of soft curly hair on her forehead that they call a widow's peak. It is believed that a woman with a widow's peak outlives her husband. Hope did just that because she took no nonsense from any man—especially not from some old drunk first thing in the morning.

"What kind a foolishness you telling the child?" she yelled at the top of her lungs. "As a matter of fact, who him belong to is none of your business."

"Eh eh, why you so sharp this morning," the old man responded calmly.

"Just take your Bay Rum and go home. This boy has work to do around here."

The old man winked at Roderick, opened the bottle of Bay Rum, and poured it down his throat in one big gulp. He shook his head vigorously at the sharpness of the brew. This startled Roderick because he knew that his mother only used Bay Rum to rub him down when he was sick. She called it the magic of the spirits. He never saw anyone drink it before. For the rest of the day Roderick wondered about this strange man who knew so much about his mother and spoke such strange things.

Roderick's crude quarters was the old storage room situated at the end of the long corridor leading to the back of the house. The dim light of a kerosene lamp on a night stand cast ghostly shadows of barrels, boxes and burlap bags piled high to the ceiling. The walls were off-white and the peeling paint exposed a rusty burgundy coat that told its age. A print of the Madonna and Child, which seemed centuries old, hung in full view. On the far corner, next to the window, a pair of old dirty grownup's trousers hung most entitled on a rusty nail with a leather belt that dangled from its waist. An old army cot was pushed flush against the west wall and it was draped with a brown and green plaid cotton sheet. At the head of the cot was a bundle of old clothes that formed a pillow. The flooring was gray and white polka dot terrazzo tiles that displayed the residue of brown floor wax between the symmetrical designs, weather-worn cracks, and creases. On the floor beside the cot was a torn shirt that was folded to form a bedside mat. A mahogany cabinet void of display windows stood in its antiquity behind the door. Its shelves were neatly stocked with black, red, and brown shoe polish, bathing soaps of all kinds, exercise books, pens, pencils, and all sorts of knick knacks.

Roderick looked around in wonder, "This could never be where Auntie a put me to sleep tonight. Nobody don't live so!" He placed his grip with his clothes, at the foot of the cot. Then he cautiously crawled under the sheet and curled up in a fetal position. Roderick was overcome by fear of isolation, especially, since he had grown accustomed to sleeping in a large room with his brother and sister. Tonight, his circumstances had drastically changed, Olympic Gardens, 1966.

It rained all night and swift swords of lightning and deep roars of thunder kept the dogs and chickens restless. Roderick could hear rats gnawing away at flour sacks, pigtail barrels, pickled mackerel, and salt-fish boxes. It was cold and damp. He thought about his comfortable bed in the country and the days he would spend down by the river bathing while women washed clothes. Although he was so tired from the newness of his first hours in Kingston, falling asleep was quite a chore.

Hours into sleep time, Roderick's bladder became really heavy. He dreaded the long trek to the bathroom down the hallway that connects the shop to the rest of the house. It looked like a black hole relieved only by a tiny beam of light, cast through the kitchen window from a street light. Unable to contain his water any longer, he decided to tip toe down the hallway. Aided by the very slight glow of street light, Roderick ran his hand along the wall to guide his steps. He moved swiftly past two closed doors. He could hear a snoring chorus that sounded like an immense clanging of pots and pans. His cousins were in lunar bliss.

Suddenly, something came crashing down and he thought that he would die. His heart started to race out of time and he broke out into a cold sweat. Then he heard a squeaky sound like the wooden floor was shifting beneath his feet. He froze. "Lawd a massi!" he whispered within the mysteries of the dark. A warm breath puffed over his thin neck. Something tickled his face and his raw animal instinct made him swing his hands that got tangled in a long string. On trying to untangle the string, Stephen stretched his hands over and pulled the string and the light came on. There it was—a huge ceramic pot of African Violets in splinters on the ground. It was ruined, and the plant ripped from the soil. If Roderick had taken one step further, the broken pot would have ripped into his flesh, causing serious injury. By now, Roderick had forgotten that he wanted to pee. He hurried to clean up the mess hoping to put it together again.

Stephen said in a loud whisper, "Look what you do."

"I swear, I never see it…it…it did dark and a boungse down the vase," Roderick whispered.

"I will help you, but you have a lot of explaining to do."

"Thank you…what you name was again?""Stephen man." He shared a smile as the light glowed against his pale cheeks revealing slight freckles below both eyes.

"Gwaan go use the toilet. Mi wi wait fi yuh."

Roderick breathed a sigh of relief, took a pee and went back to his quarters. To Roderick, Stephen seemed kind of cool in his hand painted *Rocksteady with Alton and Eddie* tee shirt with cut off sleeves. Barefooted, he stood nearly six feet tall.

Roderick lay awake counting stars through a broken windowpane, listening to his rodent roommates, and ruminating about his first day in Olympic Gardens. Although his cousin tried to make him comfortable about the accident with Hope's shattered ceramic pot—he worried about his impending doom in the morning. He was restless and could not fall asleep. Then his mind reflected on the old man. He recounted how that strange, nameless man told him that he would have to employ three tactics to buy his freedom, of which, the first was prayer. At that moment, he prayed, and hit his pillow three times, and was soon fast asleep.

Next morning before the rooster crowed, Aunt Hope stormed through the John Crow-beaded curtain that hung by the door of Roderick's makeshift quarters. "This is not a holiday boy. You will make yourself useful around here. I see you break mi good ceramic vase already. I had this heirloom in our family before you were born. I can see we are going to have problems. I will let this slip this time, but watch your step with me, you hear me! You not gwine drive me outa my mind like you been doing to my sister. You understand boy!"

"Yes maam," he replied with his eyes to his chest as he moved quickly to the kitchen."

"I guess that everywhere mi go, problem follow mi," he thought to himself. Thank heavens she never hit me in mi head like mi madda. She much nicer than my madda or it must be last night prayers that save mi this time," he wondered.

As the sun rose, the rest of the clan started to scamper for the bathroom in preparation for school. There was loud chatter. They were hurling accusations about missing pencils and boogers. By then, Roderick had washed the kitchen floor and was busy helping Aunt Hope with the breakfast. The children ate and said goodbye to Roderick. It was his turn to have breakfast, alone. After breakfast, he took the plates to the kitchen area, a little open-air walkway off the shop that was partially covered by an awning. The sink faced the front of the neighbor's yard. Just then, he saw the little girl with bright eyes all dressed in her school uniform with her leather bag on her shoulder. She looked smart with her navy blue ribbons at the end of her two ponytails. She smiled at him but he was too sad to reciprocate. Everyone seemed to be going to school except him. He held back an unforced silent tear.

~ゆ)

That evening, just before his cousins came home, the little girl ran straight from the bus stop into the shop. She almost knocked over Miss

Dillon's basket of fruits, which she sold on the landing of the piazza.

"Little girl, watch where you going!" yelled Miss Dillon.

"Sorry Miss," she respectfully replied. The little girl came to buy candy, but more especially, to get a better look at her new neighbor now waiting to serve her behind the counter. To the girl, he looked around eleven and tall for his age. His copper-toned skin was soft and his round eyes were greenish blue. He had sand brown hair, strong looking white teeth. Roderick seemed happy to see the girl and he welcomed her, warmly. He had been serving nosey old women all day who asked way too many questions. She was like a breath of fresh air.

"Serve me a paradise plum and two mint balls, please," the girl ordered.

"Yes maam."

"Don't call me maam. I have a name. Chloe—Chloe Goodman. That's my name. What is your name?"

"My name is Roderick, maam."

"Don't call me maam ah say. I bet I am your age."

"How you know my age, maam? That will be penny ha' penny."

"There you go again calling me maam. I can see we are going to have problems."

"Problems! It look like everybody a Kingston ha problem," he mumbled.

"I don't have any problems yah boy. Tell me, what brings you here?"

"Why you want to know?"

"Just curious."

"Curious? Yuh jus faas. Mi madda say, curious puppy lose dem nose."

"Excuse the rush," she lashed back.

"Yuh jus like di ole ooman dem dat come here today."

"I look old to you? This is not the right way to get to know someone, Chloe" she thought to herself. "Let's try again. How come you with Miss Hope?"

"Mi madda sen me to live wit her."

"Why?"

"Kingston people ask question eh! If you really must know. Is a long story. "

"I like stories," she said in a facetious manner. "A fling the wood hangle hairbrush and lik mi likkle sister. It bruk her nose right in two before it land straight through mi madda vanity mirror."

"What got you so mad," she pressed.

Roderick seemed to be losing his composure, "Si yah, noh ask me no more question…me look mad to you?"

"I'd better leave him alone, he must really have a temper," Chloe deliberated in the privacy of her mind, but insisted.

"Gwaan, tell me more!"

"Esther say mi dunce."

"Who is Esther?"

"Mi likkle sista. She always hear mi madda cuss mi how mi dunce, so she tek it up pan herself fi call mi soh.

"True true?"

"Yes. Nuff time mi madda talk in front a her say if mi si mi name pan a bulla cake mi wouldna know it—mi just born dunce. Mi neva out fi tek it so dis time so mi fling di brush after her. Then mi madda get bex and pack mi tings, put me pan Missa Gilford old country bus with all dem frowsy people, and send me come to Aunt Hope. Satisfy now?"

"You right. Is a long story for true," Chloe said.

He had recited his story without a hitch. Somewhere in Chloe's mind she was convinced that maybe there was more to Roderick's story.

Roderick did not want to expose the straw that really broke the camel's back; instead, he told the girl an older story that was not as painful as the bloody beating he received after sending Esther flying down the hill, leaving her with broken body parts. His eyes were turning red and Chloe could not begin to understand the pain he must feel.

"So why didn't you go to school this morning?"

"You ask plenty questions ee? Everything a tell you is the truth a telling you." He hissed his teeth real loud, almost in disgust. "What mek mi think yuh woulda understand mi anyway? Penny ha' penny please, miss. Don't mek a ask you again or it will be sixpence."

She handed him the coins and smiled. "Sounds like your mother is the one who needs to get put on a bus and sent far away, not you," she thought to herself. "Look at those tender eyes," she smiled deep inside her heart. Chloe gave yet another generous smile and said, "I have to go now. See you tomorrow?"

"Yes, see you tomorrow. But promise me. Don't ask me no more question. All right?"

"Tomorrow. Ok?" She snapped her finger, placed her hands under her armpits, rocked her head from side to side, and then scratched the floor with her right foot as if to reincarnate the funky chicken dance.

It was getting busy in the shop. Children were anxious to buy Miss Hope's grater cake, which she made fresh every Tuesday, and to take a peek at the new boy in town. As Chloe said goodbye to him, his heart pounded with delight. "At least somebody wanted to know about me," and he made an about turn straight into Aunt Hope's two tons of breasts.

"Listen noh, me never bring you here to hobnob with mi customer dem. Chloe is a decent little girl. She comes from good family. Me and

Mr. Goodman never have no fuss yet, so try don't make no problem for mi," she scolded as her voice rose to a piercing screech.

"There we go again, that word, problem," he could only think to himself.

*Chapter Three*

## What Shall I Do With This Fellow

The early morning sun sat on his head with a vengeance. To Roderick, any minute now, his sand brown hair would ignite from the heat. He had been washing the piazza and the sidewalk with Jeyes all-purpose disinfectant, where last night's love-struck dogs' stinking filth and urine was now a colony of flies. When he finished, he opened the shop door to welcome the first customers. He had learned how to weigh flour, sugar, cornmeal and salt really well after many a reprimand from his aunt. Once Roderick learned, there was nothing that could stop him. "I am the best sugar wrapper in town," he once told Miss Dillon. One thing he did not like was cutting up the salt pork. It stank! The brine often got into his eyes and was murder on a gaping sore.

Slowly and reluctantly, Roderick was trying to fit into his new experience. It was three months since he had come into town. He missed home with all its natural beauty, wide open fields, rugged terrain, river, sea, birds, and animals. He had no friends except the fisherman in the village whom he called Uncle. Town was cluttered with houses and people. Fumes from buses and cars made it hard to breathe especially around eight o'clock in the morning when traffic competed for space in the heat. There were frequent fights in the neighborhood. Children fought. Lovers fought. Friends fought, often punctuated by colorful bad words uttered with passion and malice, more often than not, having something to do with women's underclothes. Most men hated to be called those words. If you wanted to get a young man upset in Town just cuss him with one of those words. Many had died in this town because of bad words. The courts even charged you a fee for cursing.

Young Madden loved to cuss and call down fire and brimstone on his family and neighbors who did not agree with his ideologies. Twice in one month, the police raided his home where he lived with his parents. It was rumored that he had refused to go to school, he had found a new culture, a new religion. He was a Rastafarian. Young Madden did not cut his hair, drank no alcohol, ate no pork, and swore by the King James Version of the Holy Bible and The Sixth and Seventh Books of Moses. Suraj told Roderick that the young man followed some of the precepts of his ancestors—the Sikh people of Punjab, a state in northwest India. Young Madden practiced some of their dietary ways. The old man did not seem to have a problem understanding the young Madden because he truly believed that all religious paths led to ultimate liberation and one true god. Tell that to Father Madden. He was convinced that his son had gone mad, professing Emperor Haile Selassie of Ethiopia to be the supreme King of Kings and Lord of Lords. Mr. Madden was a devout Anglican and a loyal civil servant. He was not prepared to have his son bring any disgrace on his family by posing as some ganja-smoking, nappy-headed saddhu—turning his house into a Nyabinghi campground. He was not having any of that. Lessons like these fascinated Roderick and he was becoming fond of the old man.

Roderick and Chloe were enjoying each other's company, although they were from different sides of the fence. Chloe could not wait to get home in the afternoons so that she could buy candy at the shop;

this gave her a chance to see Roderick. He could not wait to see her, as long as he did not displease his aunt. He was a smart boy but he spent so much time scrubbing floors, weeding the yard, working in the kitchen, and sometimes slaving over a big tub of his cousins' dirty clothes. Chloe never liked Roderick's relatives except for his cousin, Stephen. He seemed like an easygoing boy. The other one was lazy and loud. She became very concerned that Roderick did not go to school like the rest of the boys.

"This is so unfair. What a price to pay for a broken nose and a mirror!" she would say to herself. "There's got to be a way to make somebody change their mind about his punishment. If only I could get a chance to have him all to myself, we could figure out a way." This became a recurring thought, eventually growing into an obsession for Chloe, but she had no one to tell. Weeks passed and she could not come up with an answer. "If only I could get him to myself, perhaps we could come up with a real plan." Then one day, Chloe had her epiphany—a very bright idea. "Perhaps I should ask my dad's permission to lend Roderick some of my old books." Her thoughts ran wild like the magical yellow love bush that invaded the hibiscus hedges growing by her gate. She soon built up her courage to ask her dad.

"Paradise plum!" she thought. Chloe ran into the living room where dad was doing his crossword puzzle. "Can I get some money to buy paradise plum at the shop?"

"Oh sure. Remember, too many sweets spoil teeth."

"Yes Daddy." Without delay, she ran to the shop. When she arrived, she saw Roderick making change for a customer. Chloe started tapping her feet edgily because it seemed as if he was spending too much time on this transaction. Her thoughts were so loud that Roderick could almost hear them. "Hurry up noh!"

"Hi Chloe."

"Hi. Listen. A have a bright idea. A going to lend you some of my books so you can have something to read. But listen, your auntie mustn't know. A going to leave them one-at-a-time behind the dumpster at the front. You can always find them there. Promise?"

"Promise. When?"

"Starting tonight."

"Tonight! You crazy!" he retorted. "Duppy and rolling calf walk like man a night time."

"No. You crazy. Nothing don't name duppy. Just pick up the books in the morning."

"Awright, but remember that when you going back into your house in the night, duppy might follow you. Just walk backwards into your house so you can face the duppy at the door. Is true! When dem see you face dem not gwine want to come inside."

"You know what…I better leave now because this duppy story is foolishness."

"Foolinish You think is foolinish. Gwaan. Auntie coming," he whispered.

"Bye."

She ran out the door with glee almost tripping over the customer who was entering the shop.

"That little gal in here often. You better watch it you hear me," his aunt chided. This was no time for a response from Roderick. His attention quickly shifted to the patron who had walked in and, who called out, "Serve."

"Can I help you, maam?"

Lent was approaching and so Aunt Hope made sure that her house and the surroundings were squeaky clean. She got rid of the clutter and Roderick was very useful during those days. It was the most important time of the year for some Christians on the island. Although Roderick had no knowledge of its significance, Hope made sure she tried to convert him. She told him that he would have to go to mass with them, place ashes on his forehead, and ask God to forgive him of all the bad things he had done that year.

The day before Ash Wednesday, Roderick got up early because he had a lot of chores. Aunt Hope and the boys were going to mass the next morning and they had to look real sharp. Roderick had to use a coal iron to press their white shirts, pants, and handkerchiefs. Then, he had to clean their shoes, and make sure they had matching socks and ties. He resented having to do all this work especially for Nelton. Roderick believed that he was unfairly punished by Aunt Hope for all the scrapes Nelton dragged him into; she felt Nelton was always right. Nelton liked to pick a fight and Roderick never backed away from one, especially when he knew that he was right. In any case, he worked diligently all day long. When he completed his tasks, he joined his aunt in the shop. He washed the floors and restocked the shelves while she poured cherry syrup in swirly patterns on warm grater cakes. He never quite understood why Aunt Hope did not enlist the other boys to help out with the chores. "Dem is just a spoil lazy lot," he once told Chloe. "This is real hard. Why mama send me weh come work like Maas Tom old mule?" he protested. Roderick was tired and wished that he could just run away. But there was nowhere to hide in the crowded city that seemed to have more buildings than trees. Then he recalled the old man telling him that it would not be easy to become free unless he worked hard. That night he knelt at the foot of his cot and prayed:

*Dear God.*

*You know I am not a bad boy. I don't deserve this bad hangling. Please God. Let my mama take me back and give me one more chance. You know how much me fraid a rat. Please to make mama love me. Bless Kloweey. Bless Steevin. And though a can't stand Niltan, bless Niltan too. Bless the old man. Make me strong so I can work hard. God the father. God the son. God the Holy Spirit. Amen.*

Holy Week and Mr. Goodman stayed home from work that Good Friday although he never celebrated Christian holidays. Instead, he would send Chloe to church with his sister-in-law who was an ardent Catholic. Mr. Goodman's ancestors came to Jamaica during the Spanish Inquisition. Although he was not a religious man, he often went to the United Congregation of Israelites Synagogue Shaare Shalom on High Holy days. This was a tradition that was kept in his family and inculcated in him by his grandmother who he affectionately called, Ma Bubbie. She was a great storyteller who often spoke of her great grandparents' life in Spain. How her family helped to form districts in an effort to preserve their Jewish identity under the Catholic orthodoxy. She would take great care to tell him stories of families that were banished from their homes and how they relied on the goodness of strangers.

Mr. Goodman recounts one such story of a little boy who woke up one morning and his parents had disappeared. He wondered the streets looking for them for an entire day. Then he became very hungry. He knocked on several doors and all the neighbors seemed to have vanished. The little boy was petrified and convinced that he was going to die of hunger on the streets of Barcelona. As the sun was setting, he curled up on the steps of an old burned out building waiting for death to come. Just before he closed his eyes, he saw a beautiful girl in a burgundy dress with long sleeves, and the lace of her petticoat swayed gracefully around her ankles. Her head was covered with a beautiful scarf that fell slightly around her neck. She had a basket in her hands.

On reaching the boy, she handed him the basket. When he lifted the lid, there was bread, figs, and water. He looked up to say thanks, but she had disappeared. Sometimes, help comes from the most unlikely sources and at the most difficult times. Ma Bubbie always told him, "Value the life of the stranger as your own. Never turn your head away from the destitute. Be an instrument of love." This is one of the many stories that shaped Mr. Goodman's life. He was proud to be a part of the only congregation in the western hemisphere in which the Ashkenazi, Sephardic, Reconstructionists, Zionists, and Jamaicans who embraced Judaism, worship together in peace and harmony. The synagogue even has an original dirt floor and is considered authentic, holy to the Jewish people. Mr. Goodman was proud of the Jewish contribution to Jamaican life, and was especially grateful for the spiritual and moral guidance, as well as, the public personae of Rabbi Bernard Hooker, a caring man.

Today, Chloe offered to stay home with her dad and make him breakfast in bed. Her dad was surprised at the gesture seeing the little girl never missed Good Friday with her Aunt Frances.

"You look like you could do with a little help in the kitchen this morning."

"No Dad, I want to do this myself." She got the pillows and propped his feet up. "You just relax." Chloe prepared hard-boiled eggs, hard-dough bread with butter, and served up a treat of mint tea from choice leaves in her garden. Her father kept up the small garden next to the mango tree as a memorial to her mother who died of stomach cancer. Her mom believed that tilling the garden was one of the best ways she could relax and keep her mind off the sickness. She loved nature's bloom.

"This is perfect," Chloe deliberated. I have Dad all to myself and so I can talk to him about Roderick." Chloe knew that she could always get her dad's attention when it came to matters of education—reading, writing, and arithmetic. He was an erudite and cultured man, a quiet and gentle giant who studied the dictionary and was never seen without his Roget's Thesaurus. He read avidly and often rewarded Chloe for reading at least five new books each month. Now she liked to read so much she couldn't wait to share it with someone she thought less fortunate than her: Roderick.

"This is a great meal," Dad said with admiration. "You will be a fine cook someday my *shana maidel*." He affectionately referred to Chloe as his *shana maidel*, a Yiddish term of endearment for a pretty girl. The girl's gesture sort of puzzled her dad, but he never let on that he figured she was up to something.

"Thank you, Dad. I always wanted to do something special for you. Oh, by the way, have you ever talked to the little boy that moved in next door? His name is Roderick."

"Yes I have. Just 'howdy' on one or two occasions when I stopped by to purchase the newspaper. He seems to be quite a handy fellow."

"Have you noticed that he has not been to school since he got here? He just works and works and works, Dad."

"No, I hardly noticed. He just seems to have a lot of manners and works at his chores."

"Well Dad, I was thinking—

"Don't think too much my dear," and he patted her gently on her head.

"Could you ask Miss Hope if I could lend Roderick some of my books? He cannot read very well. So maybe you could teach him to read too."

"How do you know Roderick cannot read? He works in a shop— he must be quite capable." Mr. Goodman, concerned about interfering in his neighbor's affairs, told Chloe that it was not their place to make that choice. She was crushed but she would never challenge her dad or disobey him. They lived a simple, uncomplicated life. She knew how much her dad stressed the importance of education. For now, this was Chloe's mêlée, a private conflict that she had to solve alone. She spent the rest of Good Friday contemplating her next move.

It was a starless, pitch-black night. The air was still and the night was hot. Chloe could feel the sweat running down her cotton nightie sleeves. In quiet desperation, she lay awake consulting her favorite patterns in her ceiling for answers. "Van Gogh! What shall I do? / Kapo! You have always been true. / Wordsworth! Tell me of mirth / Oh clever Longfellow! / tell me what to do for this fellow?" Well, Longfellow was the only one who replied because he always stayed up late at night.

"Lend Roderick some books so he can learn of great men!"

That was all Chloe needed to hear. He confirmed what she had been thinking all along. Forthwith, she tip-toed to her bookcase across from her bed, and packed a paper bag with some very special books she wanted to share, especially those that had no real girl heroes: *Robinson*

*Crusoe* by Daniel Defoe, *Memoirs of a Midget* by Walter de la Mare, *The Three Musketeers* by Alexandre Dumas. They were among the first she parted with. Then she put on her robe and tied her head to protect her from the night air—just as her mother taught her to do. Then she walked softly and carefully toward the backdoor. She unlocked it without her dad hearing, and went out into the yard. Most young children on the island had a skewed view of the mysteries of the night, a kind of nyctophobia from the duppy stories of their ancestors; Chloe would brave this night.

Out of the blue, the neighbor's dogs started to make a strange howl, "aoooo...aoooo...aoooo" — a sign that someone was going to die, so the people said. Her heart started to pound. She could hardly breathe. A firefly flickered its luminescent tail lights in spiraling circles along the path. The girl smiled. She was only a few steps away from the garbage pan on the side of the shop that she had staked out earlier as the perfect place to deposit the books. "Could there be someone lurking in the dark? Nah," she consoled herself. "No one would even imagine that I am out here." Although Chloe harbored private feelings of fear of the dark, fear of rolling calves, fear of the wooden-foot man, and fear of the black-heart man, she knew her friend Longfellow was always with her.

# Chapter Four

# Five and Five a Ten Me and You a Fren

Morning. The sun was brilliant in the sky and cool northeast trade winds were blowing through her hair. Chloe could smell the peach-flavored shampoo her dad used to wash her hair the day before. As she pushed the gate to hurry to the bus stop down the road, a small stone fell at her feet. Turning around, she saw Roderick bent down behind his gate. He waved the paper-bag with the books she had placed behind the garbage pan the night before. All the while she was praying that the stray dogs would not get to them before he did. He smiled and mouthed, "Thank you. I have something for you." He pointed to a huge stone beside the gate where he had placed a note on a piece of torn brown paper bag. Chloe quickly retrieved it and hastily put it in her side pocket, and then she rushed to get on the bus that was arriving. She was curious as to what was written on the paper.

The bus was hot and packed with all the seats taken. She put her bag snug between her feet on the floor and held on to the back of the seat in front of her with one hand. Chloe was careful not to crush the starched white collar of the distinguished gentleman reading the morning news from the Daily Gleaner. Between her thumb and index finger, on her other hand, she unfolded the paper and started to read:

*The Slo Fool by Roderick*
*There was a pore boy*
*Dem take for one toy*
*Him have no fren atawl*
*Some time him jus fi ball*
*Him teacha say him slo*
*Madda say you have to go*
*Him meet one girl name Kloweey*
*But I do not know what rime with Kloweey so I stop here so.*

At the end of the poem, he drew the most beautiful bird her eyes had ever seen. It was as if he had drawn his signature. "What a beautiful poem," the girl thought. "But he expresses himself so well. So how come they say he is slow?" The poem sort of made her sad. And so that evening, she gave Roderick a copy of a poem she had written when she was nine years old.

<u>*When Nature Stops*</u>
*By Chloe Goodman*

*I like to hear the sound of night*
*And watch the fireflies in flight*
*I like to listen to the crickets sing*
*For I don't worry about a thing.*

*And when the rain begins to fall*
*I hear the children's silly call*
*Come out everybody and let us play*
*Because there is no school today.*

*But then the rain stops suddenly*
*And sunshine wake flowers gleefully*
*And slushy puddles just disappear*
*I sit by my window and shed a tear.*

From that day onward, the children traded poems, they traded stories, and they traded drawings. Roderick remembered on one of Suraj's visits that the old man told him 'poetry is from God.'

"A wonder if dis is a poem from God. Me never hear from God before?" Roderick questioned. He continued to draw more lovely pictures and left most of the poetry to the girl. Nature informed his art and his pictures told stories about life in the country, of many adventures down by the river, pictures of the wide open fields of yams, cassava, mangos, and bananas. And when his imagination was running wild, you could almost hear the horses, as if on battle fields. The more he etched his thoughts and feelings on paper or on any surface he could find, the more his fears and anguish came into view.

"A gwine tell mama pan yuh!" The annoying sound of Nelton's voice jeered through the crack in the gate. "Yuh know that yuh not suppose to trouble Mr. Goodman daughter."

"A not troublin her...mine yuh business," Roderick replied angrily.

Nelton used both legs to create a wedge in the gate so that Roderick could not pass. This infuriated Roderick because he did not want Aunt Hope to see him away from his post.

"Get outa mi way or a gwine kick yuh down," snapped Roderick with teeth tightly clenched.

"Kick me noh...since you so bad...kick me," Nelton provoked.

"A seh to move outa mi way!" Roderick tried to control his temper but Nelton would not allow him. Nelton knew that his mother would never reprimand him for any scrapes between he and Roderick.

"I never did like you anyway!" Roderick retorted. He pushed his body against the gate to get inside and somehow he squeezed Nelton's leg between the gate and the wall. Whoop! Boof! Boofum! Nelton punched him in the face and Roderick's bag with the books spilled on the ground. He became so irate that he knocked Nelton to the ground with a slap. Boof! Dum! The cousins wrestled but Nelton was no match for Roderick. By now he had become so incensed that he pinned Nelton against the wall.

"Let me go…see how you dirty up mi uniform…fool!" screamed Nelton.

"Is me wash it," Roderick replied with a right hand sock to Nelton's mouth.

"Mama! Mama! Fool fool boy. Get off me. Get off!"

"Don't ever fool with me again," Roderick warned, pulled himself away from Nelton, and hastily secured his prized books that seemed to hold life's mysteries. Aunt Hope was just in time to see Roderick pulling himself away from Nelton only to reveal her son's bloody mouth. When she saw her child bleeding, and his messy uniform, she grabbed Roderick by the collar.

Without any questions, she draped him up by the shirt, took off her shoe, and started to beat Roderick anywhere on his body the shoe landed. She beat him on his head and back. Somehow, Roderick managed to let go of his shirt in her hands and speedily ran away. He climbed the mango tree next to the outhouse with one hand clutching his parcel, and then he sat on a limb. Rivers of sweat bathed his body as he panted almost out of breath. All he could hear was his Aunt Hope petting Nelton, saying how sorry she was for bringing this problem into their house.

"As soon as I can get a hold of his mother, he is going back to country. Brush off your clothes, wash your face, take some warm salt water and rinse out your mouth. The bus will be coming down the road soon and you don't want to be late for school."

Roderick did not know what to make of Aunt Hope's irrational behavior. He just stroked the books for clues. "Beating inna di country—

beating inna di town; Lawd a when dis beating a goh done?"

Roderick stayed up in the tree for most of the morning. He thought about a lot of things. He marveled at the strangeness of Aunt Hope's toes when she took off her shoe. Her first toe was extraordinarily longer than the big toe. Then he remembered Uncle telling him that it is a sign that the woman will not only beat her husband, she will rule him. Roderick dozed off once or twice between the sound of dogs barking at cars and pedestrians. At one time, he looked up on a branch that hung lazily above him and he spotted what seemed like an odd looking green mango—elongated by the glare of the sun. He shook the sleep out of his eyes to get a steadier gaze at this anomaly. Then it started to move unprovoked by the wind. "Why did you fight back?"

"Yuh talking to me?" Roderick replied.

"Yes…you. Why did you bloody the boy's nose?"

"Is him start it…him block mi from pass the gate."

"Couldn't you have gone by way of the shop?"

"A never want Auntie to see mi wid the book dem. She would tink mi tief dem or somethin and tek dem way from me. For like she don't want to see mi read…only work," Roderick defended his actions.

"But why did you feel the need to fight the boy?"

Roderick came back impatiently, "Him call mi fool fool and mi just tiad a him a trouble mi all the time."

"Trouble you?"

"Yes, him trouble mi too much for him know him madda not goin say nothin."

"Blood is thicker than water—our allegiance to our family is sometimes stronger no matter how negatively we feel towards them. Fighting never solves anything, friend."

"Fren…who fren?"

"I call you friend because I learned long ago that you must seek a friend before you need a friend."

"Mi don't understand what yuh mean by that."

"Did it dawn on you that perhaps Nelton wants to be your friend?"

"Is mi cousin…not mi fren! Chloe is my fren," he emphasized with confidence.

"Boys will be boys. They tend to play rough most of the times."

"Play rough! Then me a what. Me a boy to. And me don't trouble him. Yuh unreasonable yuh know. Yuh want them fi just batta batta mi all di time and mi jus teck it soh? Me have feelings yuh know."

"Remember, two wrongs don't make a right, friend."

"Suraj tell me to do unto others as me would have them do unto me—and so him punch me and me punch him back."

"I hardly think that is what Suraj meant. You should always strive to do good so that others can be good to you."

"But all I do from I come inna dis hot miserable Kingston is good to de whole family a dem."

"How long have you been here now…seven months?"

"How you know so much…then is why him not kind back to me like Chloe?"

"The little girl is nice to you, and you are kind to her because somehow you figured out one day in the shop that good fences make good neighbors."

"You just a talk all kinda talk this morning."

"No, friend. You must learn to take the bitter with the sweet, learn to balance the bad things that cause you pain with those things that bring you happiness."

"Mi don't understand a word yuh a say to me."

"You two will remain at loggerheads until something bad happens. You can catch more flies with honey than vinegar because it is much simpler to get the boy on your side in a kinder and gentler manner than imitating his unfriendly ways."

"Mi don't have to like him at all."

"An old toady told me once long ago, laugh, and the world laughs with you—weep, and you weep alone."

Roderick was convinced he was not getting anywhere with this line of argument. "Is what dis?" Roderick could see much clearer now and realized that the strange fruit was a bluish green lizard. The reptile winked its slow heavy eyelids, swung its tail over the branch, and morphed with the green leaves and brown twigs. This startled the young boy who was beginning to feel quite famished. He couldn't imagine that he was so deeply engaged in a conversation with a bare-faced green lizard.

"A mus really hungry fi true," he thought to himself. "Is mus be one dead somebody duppy Aunt Hope dem plant a de foot a dis mango tree. A better come down now."

Roderick assumed that his Aunt Hope had cooled off and so he mustered up some courage, slid down the trunk of the tree, scraped his tummy. Yet, he dragged himself onto the piazza where Miss Dillon was just packing away the leftovers from her breakfast. He stood there for a few moments and she felt his presence. She turned around and saw in his countenance that something was wrong; she saw hunger in his eyes. With great care, she gave him the food and a fresh, purple, ripe star apple. The two exchanged no words.

Roderick intended to ease back into the shop where Aunt Hope was engaged with a customer—hoping desperately that she had forgotten the fight earlier that morning. When, along came a young man who could be about eighteen years old. His gait was broad, and his stride was long. He wore straight-legged dark pants that had a slight shimmer against the sun. His tee shirt was etched with an eye-catching portrait of the much talked about Trinidadian-born revolutionary Stokely Carmichael whose bright bulging eyes were his most striking features. The young man's locks flowed gracefully past his shoulders and he covered his crown with a knitted tam of red, green, and gold.

"Mawnin Miss Dillon," the polite young man brought greetings.

"Mawnin Master Madden," Miss Dillon replied with a welcoming smile.

"You know my usual—afu, fresh green and ripe bananas, plenty igitebles, ilalloo; okra, red peas, and leggo a small bottle of the good molasses." Roderick stared at the young man with awe and thought to himself, "Is must be him Maas Suraj tell me about."

"Hail the youtman," Madden said.

"Hello," Roderick replied.

"Why is thy countenance so fixed upon I and I?"

Roderick stuttered, "No...no...nothing sir."

"No sir business. Lij Tafari Garvey is I name...don't follow Miss Dill and them weh call I Madden. That name was imposed upon I and I...I don't deal wid mad business."

Miss Dillon threw her head back with an outburst of laughter. She always found the young man's speech amusing—the way he changed the words to suit his own philosophy.

"So why the youtman not in school today?"

"Dem don't sen me go a school. I am the shop boy."

"Is so dem tell you. You a shop boy? Well dem don't know any better still...for dem people weh call you shop boy learn that inna the downpressor school still. But the youtman need some basic foundation that dem schools can't give anyway."

"Wha yuh mean?"

"In your spare time you need to read your Bible."

"Mi doh have spare time...me doh have Bible."

"Well, a goin get you one."

"No, no…my Aunt Hope doh really want me to tek nothing from people. My fren Chloe give me some books and me have to hide dem from her."

"Such atrocity! Blood and fire fi di wicked."

"Eh em," Miss Dillon interrupted sharply, clearing her throat, having spotted Miss Hope approaching the trio. Hope grabbed Roderick by the waist of his pants, hoisting him off the ground, much to his discomfort.

"Listen to me boy—you have work to do around here. We don't need them kind a nappy-head, ganja-smoking people roun we family. You just hawl yuself inside. You don't need them sort a friend," Hope scornfully scolded.

"Blood and fire pan Sister Hopeless. I did not come to you," Lij lashed back. "Oonu is oppressors of young intellect. Let I man have I goods Miss Dillon." He took the bag of provisions from her, turned to Roderick, looked steadfast in his eyes, pointing his index fingers upwards, he said, "Soon you will find out the man you are supposed to be."

# Chapter Five

# Baby Face

The mud was piling up where the zinc roof's gutter emptied torrential July rain showers behind the outhouse next to the three-story chicken coop and barble dove cage. It had been raining steadily for several days, and gale-force winds swept across the island threatening to ruin every home, all livestock, and every food crop in its path. Roderick's over-sized galoshes could hardly support him from the suction of the slushy, muddy ground as he struggled to get the first brown eggs of the day. It was cold and wet and the hens seemed rather unfriendly today. Without disturbing the sitting hens, he filled a basket of large warm eggs some of which would grace the table at breakfast, later that morning.

Chloe had grown accustomed to waking up early. Many a morning she would just sit by her window watching the daylight illuminate Roderick into full view. Some days, she would watch painfully as he dragged his half-a-sleep tired body to the standpipe to wash his face with the first cold, morning water. He seemed almost content with his situation at times, but Chloe knew that he would prefer to be involved in the activities that children his age enjoyed. "Hard work seemed to agree with him," she thought for a cynical moment. Yet, nothing stopped her preoccupation with the day he would go to school again.

At times like these, Chloe really missed the tenderness of her mother. She was only seven when her mother died yet she knew that her mother would not be unkind to any child in her care. Unlike her mom, Miss Hope seemed utterly cruel and showed partiality to her incorrigible sons. To the girl, good people died way before they were honored for their kind deeds.

Summer was here and schools were closed for the holidays. Three weeks leading up to Independence Day, which has been celebrated on the sixth of August, since 1962, Aunt Hope's piazza was set up like a bazaar, an open marketplace. Higglers and artisans from the neighborhood spread their wares on straw mats and some hung them from mobile stalls. The astute shopper could find anything: wooden craft, straw mats, bags, national flags, memorabilia, crocheted doilies of elaborate styles especially the pineapple and rose petal patterns, leather sandals, dolls, dried coconut, calabash ware, soup bowls, bags, earrings, and jewel cases. You name it—the artisans made it. Their display was a colorful commercial zone of culture and national pride. Festival songs filled the people with euphoria as they celebrated their emancipation from the jaws of colonial encroachment.

Miss Dillon's transistor radio was the centerpiece for entertainment on the piazza. For years, during the daytime hours, she listened faithfully to American radio drama serial imports like *Doctor Paul* and *Portia Faces Life*. Although she never knew a real lawyer, she found it quite intriguing that Portia was a woman who had to balance life at home and work. Somehow, Miss Dillon could relate, having raised her children in a rocky marriage, and having to juggle getting up early to go to market. She was constantly fighting public transportation to get to anybody's piazza where she could get a spot to *cotch* and sell her provisions. It was about staying up late at night to prepare the children's school clothes, only to do the same routine all over again the next day.

Then *Dulcimina*, the island's own brand of radio drama came into her life. The daily stories captured the colorful essence of urban living with the politics that thrived at the center of island life, which kept tensions high. They made the people laugh at their struggles yet gave them hope. Every listener had a favorite character that related to some aspects of their life. Miss Dillon couldn't get enough of Ramgeet because she had to deal with quite a few *Ramgeets* when she was raising her children and could ill-afford to pay the rent. But there was something special about the festival songs; they were the equalizer, the joy to everyone on the piazza.

Most days during the festival season, disc jockeys on Radio Jamaica would play festival *Music Like Dirt*. They would play from Toots and the Maytal's *Bam Bam* to the Jamaican's *Ba Ba Boom* —the people were never tired of hearing them all day long. It was a time to do the Rocksteady whether you were rich or poor, sick, lame or lazy: Rocksteady ruled. Saturday evenings were special at the open land, where the neighborhood boys played ball most afternoons. This area transformed into a fair ground. A big Ferris wheel took center stage. Donkey rides, and rude boys' hi-fi played mostly Rocksteady and soul music from America, way into the wee hours of the morning.

Roderick was not allowed to be a part of the children's fun and excitement, except for the few times when he just ran off and allowed himself to experience the marvels of the city. Like the day he wondered off in search of the sea. He strolled along Olympic Way towards Three Miles, kicking stones and picking golden buttercups that formed pleasant oases for the bees. Then he discovered Foreshore Road.

"Shore-sea-shore…ha…this must tek mi to the sea!" He screamed. He jumped into the air, spun around like a top, and clapped his hands above his head. Then he started to run wildly like freedom gave him a gusty tailwind. The excitement he felt was like no other since he came to town. In this moment, Roderick was totally oblivious of time and space. He didn't think of asking anyone in his path for directions to the sea. Somehow, he knew that fate would take him there. Without warning, he was grounded by the piercing sounds of children, which made him stop and pay attention. Shanties—they were living in shanties, broken down shacks, makeshift squatters' quarters pieced together by zinc, timber, and any material that may withstand the heat and rain.

"Is wah dis?" Roderick said to himself. "A soh the rest a town people live?" Barefoot children. Naked children. Dirty children. Hungry looking children. Happy children. Fierce children. Screaming children coexisting in the realities of a shantytown they call home. Clearly, the boy recognized that the squalor was not fit for humans to live in, along the road that should lead him to the pristine open sea. He stared poverty and danger in the eyes and the sea seemed out of reach.

Whenever Roderick stepped out of line, Miss Hope would hammer it into his head that he should be grateful that he had a roof over his head and food to eat. In that moment, he felt lucky in a strange kind of way. His aunt never gave him pocket money like she did her sons. However, that day, having seen the devastation of the Foreshore children, Roderick decided to become enterprising. The pleasure of painting boats in the country was beginning to feel like a distant memory but Roderick was determined to preserve what little joy he could. He gathered large stones of all shapes, sizes and texture, and his paint set that Chloe had given him a month earlier. On each stone, he painted a barble dove in a cage, sitting on a black branch with green leaves and a bright golden yellow sun above. Roderick was fascinated by the beauty and strength of birds, and so he would spend many hours alone at night by the dim light making fine works of art.

He asked Miss Dillon, who was becoming his greatest ally, to see if anyone would buy them. "Maybe, somebody who like dove will buy it fi them house," he assumed.

"Boy, you really got talent," praised Miss Dillon.

"Thank you Miss Dillon."

"A can't promise you that them people will buy them. But because them so beautiful, and I like you so much, I think I will try sell them off for you."

"Thank you Miss Dillon. I could use the money to buy things for myself. Just don't mek Auntie know is for me."

"I promise." Miss Dillon smiled at Roderick's courage and inner beauty. "You are such a nice boy."

Roderick smiled back at her and ran inside with a kind of confidence and fulfillment that he had created something that someone found beautiful.

Chloe's dad had been planning for a whole month to take her to Morgan's Harbour to see the fireworks and explore the wonders of water for her upcoming science project. She wished that Miss Hope would lift Roderick's ban and let him go on the adventure with them. But Alas! Chloe was convinced that Roderick was doing better and settling in with the family. He had not been in any squabbles with the other boys lately. He worked really hard to please his Aunt Hope. Roderick hardly had free time to spare, but when he did, he reminisced about going out to sea with Uncle and the other fishermen back home. Sadly, ever since he was shipped off to Kingston, he had not heard from his family, not even on his birthday. Every time the postman came to the gate, he would hurry to see if he got any letters from them. No one wrote to him.

Father's birthday. Chloe was returning from Mrs. Lewis' garden down Booby Drive. She grew the most beautiful species of orchids and every imaginable color of Chrysanthemums in the area. The girl had just bought a bunch for her father and was on her way home. She knew how much her father loved flowers. Ever since her mother died, she became responsible for making sure that freshly cut flowers were always on the piano in the living room. This way, dad could play his favorite show songs and enjoy the aromatic flowers. She started singing, merrily skipping along:

*Dandelions gold*
*Chrysanthemums blue!*
*Buttercups bold*
*And so are you!*

As she bolted around the corner to her house, she spotted Roderick sweeping the sidewalk in front of the shop. "Perhaps a flower will brighten his day," she wondered. Without hesitation or waiting for a reaction, she gave Roderick a bright blue Chrysanthemum, then she pushed her gate open, and ran inside. Roderick was stunned. His heart began to pound deep inside his chest. He could feel and hear his sweaty merino clinging to his skin. His palms became wet and his jaw dropped open. He sniffed the flower and put it in his back pocket. Roderick kicked a mound of gravel, sending a cloud of dust in the air, and then he embraced the broom close to his chest. Instantaneously, the broom transformed right before his eyes. It was strikingly magical. The broom became the most beautiful girl in all of Olympic Gardens.

Roderick swept her off her feet and danced as he sang:

*One August mawnin'*
*I went for a walk*
*I saw my Kloweee*
*With a bunch of flowers*
*She gave me one*
*Was a pretty pretty one*
*I know, I know, I know*
*That her heart is true*
*Lawk a mi…dis ya girl a mi fren!*

That night, Roderick slept so soundly he hardly noticed that he had peed his cot. When Miss Hope went to wake him up, since he had overslept, she noticed that he was lying in a puddle of urine. She was so outraged that she flogged him. She ordered him to wash the sheets and hang them out to dry on the line. The other boys laughed at him so much that he became ashamed and embarrassed. But all that paled in comparison with the joy he felt from Chloe's thoughtfulness.

Roderick was always happy to see Maas Suraj come into the shop. Somehow Roderick felt a sense of friendship coming from this very eccentric man. Suraj had changed into a kind sage before his eyes. He was getting to like the old man a lot. As the days went by, Roderick grew more concerned about the old man's health. He had become his daytime companion and wished that he could run away with him to India.

Then one day, Roderick slipped out of the shop with a bottle of Bay Rum and two rock buns under his shirt while Miss Hope was busy tending to two of her regular customers. These were her two friends from bible study. He knew the labbrish would last for a while. He got tired of them telling him "cork your ears boy" whenever their conversations got too grown up for him. Not to mention when the radio soaps were coming on. And so, he learned to disappear as soon as they came into the shop. He handed the rum to Suraj and he followed behind him. Miss Dillon cautioned Roderick, "Don't go too far now, you hear!"

"A just going for a little walk." In no time, Roderick and Suraj were going on a stroll like kindred spirits. They passed half-finished houses, vegetable gardens, women washing clothes with babies on their backs, shirtless spirited boys played cricket with bats made from coconut bark, and dogs sleeping lazily under shade trees. A ground lizard crossed their path, and a car splashed water all over their clothes. The latter was their signal to take the shortcut that would lead to the gully bank.

Roderick turned and asked the old man a burning question he wanted to ask for some time. "Remember the other day when you come into the shop you was a talk bout Aunt Lillian, how she kind and thing?"

"Yes, she is a very kind hearted lady. I like her very much."

"What she look like?"

"Very pretty. Tall lady. Always cheerful."

"When last you see her?"

"Every now and then I visit her at her place on a Friday night. We eat, drink and have fun together, she and our friends from long time ago."

"You can take me to see her?"

"She lives far away."

"We can take the bus."

"Only if your auntie won't mind."

"Auntie will spoil everything...she won't send me anywhere. All she want me do is clean shop."

"I wouldn't say that."

"Cause you noh know!" They exchanged no words for a while.

It had rained steadily for a few days, and the gully, a muddy, eroding ditch, was still swollen with water and debris. Roderick sat on the concrete wall while Suraj sat on a piece of lumber that was suspended between a small bridge and the gully's edge. They contemplated the meaning of life as they counted broken soda bottles, cigarette boxes, old, worn out shoes, furniture, bicycle tires, tools, smelly dead fowls, small animals, and lots of memories soon forgotten. For a while, all you could hear was the gentle whisper of the wind and the birds as the two pondered in silence. Then Roderick broke the stillness.

"Have a rock bun."

"No need. The brew is just what I need to cool me off in this heat."

"Maas Suraj, if you drink too much of this Bay Rum thing you will dead!"

"Ah, young boy, death protects the mortal until the time is right."

"There you go again, talking that funny talk again." Then, there was a hush again.

"You never did finish telling me bout the war," Roderick reminded him.

"The war. The war. It was a foolish and ugly thing son. We were so young. I lost so many fellows from Australia, Africa, and my home in India, many of whom had become my friends. Some of my friends were the Jamaican soldiers from The British West Indies Regiment. We all suffered hostility at the hands of the European soldiers—we used to look out for each other. Some of my countrymen wrote and told me that upon their return to Punjab, after this Great War, life was more hellish than hell itself. It was as if they were useless, soon forgotten. I stayed in England and married my dear friend who looked after me because I was too sick to work."

"Why you call it great war?"

"Because all the big countries around the world joined in the fight."

"Oh. So where your dear friend is now?"

"Among the immortals."

"What you mean by that?"

"She lives on forever—forever in my heart."

A nervous smile formed on Roderick's face as Suraj straightened his spine on a sip of the brew.

"Tell me more about her." Roderick folded his hands across his chest and listened attentively as Suraj continued.

"Aha. She was a beautiful girl. Her skin rich like St. Catherine cocoa. Her eyes were like the stars. She was from the Maroon people of Accompong."

"What she name?"

"Her name," he said with a wide smile, "Maria Heaven. She served as a nurse in the war. My Maria was all I had. She helped me bear the pain of all my war injuries. And when my body could not handle England's cold weather, we decided to come to her home in Jamaica. Years later, her lungs became weak and she died taking care of me."

Roderick could see the tears swelling up in the old man's eyes but Suraj was too proud an old soldier to let them fall down his face.

"Oh Maas Suraj! That is a sad story."

"No son. Words cannot tell. I carry it all in my heart."

"So where is the balance of your family them?"

"I have no family son."

"So you live by yuhself?"

"I live near enough to my Maria's family, off a small pension that just keeps the breath in my body."

Roderick was almost overcome with grief and said to the old man, "You can be my family!" Then there was a very long silence. The old man glanced up at him, shook his head as if to say, *you will never understand my grief.* Moments later, Suraj tried to ease his frail body off the makeshift bench and took Roderick by his hand. "I think we should go now. Your folks might be looking for you."

"A not ready to leave yet. I want to tell you my story?"

"It's getting late." The old man acted almost dismissing, not mindful that Roderick just wanted a chance to tell his story. Then he obliged. "All right son...but make it quick. We been here long enough."

"Is a long story...it will take a whole day."

"We can't afford a whole day. Tell the story that is most on your mind right now."

"You ever feel shame so till you want to just hide way?"

"I have been ashamed in my life a few times but I never wanted to hide away."

"Well this mawning before you come a the shop, mi Aunt Hope beat mi because a mek mistake and pee pee up mi bed last night. A swear...a neva know seh a did wet di bed...she tink a spite mi do it for. Nelton pee pee up fi him bed and she neva shame him like how she shame mi this mawnin. Everybody inna di yard...every soul pan Olympic Way see mi a wash di pee pee bed sheet. Oh Mass Suraj... that noh right...it right though?"

"Children pee their bed all the time."

"But it noh right fi her fi cuss me so bad. Shame mi before people?"

"No son. Millions of children all over the world pee their beds, especially at night. I too used to pee my bed when I was a little boy." That was a surprising revelation for the boy. "I remember when I got sick during the war…I peed my bed too and somebody had to wash the sheets for me. It is natural to pee your bed especially when you are tired. You will grow it out."

"I hope that no other little children have to go through this. When I grow up…I going to make sure that no child have to feel shame like this. Miss Hope beat me for everything and she don't beat her boy dem."

"Sometimes adults can be unreasonable. They might have a lot on their minds."

"Well it look like Aunt Hope have a whole heap a things pan fi her mind all the time. No matter how hard mi try she just take it out pan me. She neva stop to think how it make me feel."

"To be kind and just is something adults learn in time. They have to grow into the shoes of justice."

"Oh Maas Suraj…you always talk dem talk what me don't understand," Roderick retorted in frustration. "What you mean by jus…what…justice?"

Suraj smiled at Roderick's childhood innocence. "When you grow up my son, you will learn that justice is something one has to cultivate—

"Like yam and banana and dem tings deh?"

"It is something one has to believe is deserving of all people. Justice has to be practiced. If you practice justice at this age, you are practicing fairness. You will treat people right."

"I can't wait to grow up…but me not goin to treat people children so."

Roderick felt a sense of *somebodiness* because Maas Suraj gave him voice to tell one of his many stories. He reached his slender hand in the brown paper bag and fetched a rock bun, which he gave to the old man, and then he took a huge hungry bite out of his bun. For the first time, Suraj allowed himself to hear the boy's cry for help, his cry for fairness, and his need to feel like other children who experience love. The pair ate within the silence that stood between them like a ferocious ancestral ghost.

The rain clouds kissed the sun forming a dark shadow that hung like a tarpaulin over their heads. It was high time for Suraj and Roderick to start their trek back home. The little boy mused about all the things the old man told him. He was not fretful that he was really in hot water with his aunt.

"Your aunt must be worried son."

Roderick did not reply. Instead, he got wrapped up in thought, "He called me son for the second time."

"We have acted irresponsibly today—now haven't we?" the old man said with a tricky smirk on his face.

"No," Roderick replied. "I can explain…Mi no fraid a her no more. She have to understand!"

"Not so my son. She does not have to understand anything you say. You must first apologize. One of the first steps to growing up is to take responsibility for your action."

"But—

"Don't but me! 'The power which you posses is but one side of the coin; the other side is responsibility. There is no power or authority without responsibility, and he who accepts the one cannot escape or evade the other,' His Imperial Majesty Emperor Haile Selassie The First, once said."

"There you go again wid yuh buss mi head word them," Roderick added.

The old man smiled because he saw a little of himself in the boy. "I remember when I was in trouble with my mother, my grandmother used to say, let us see which way the wind is going to blow."

That night, Roderick went to bed with a sore behind from Aunt Hope's tamarind switch that she sent Roderick to fetch for her. She beat him so hard that he yelled at the top of his tired lungs against the laughter and ridicule of his cousins. He screamed, "Lick mi anti but noh kill me. Mi waan goh back a country!" She beat him until she was satisfied that somehow he got the message. This time, he knew that he had spoiled his chance of going on the trip to Morgan's Harbour with Chloe and her dad. Still, that could not obliterate the wonderful day he spent on the gully edge with old man Suraj.

The girl and her dad heard Aunt Hope putting on a whipping on Roderick that night and her heart just sank into the ground. "Oh Dad," the girl said, "Why is Miss Hope so cruel to him. If she beat him so much he will really become the fool they say he is...he can't learn. She could at least send him to school!" Her dad, with eyebrows raised at her concern, chided, "Never use that word fool again."

"But Dad—

"Don't but Dad me!"

"Sorry. He has been trying hard for weeks to be good. I can't imagine what he could do to make her so cross with him."

"It must be tough on both of them my child."

"I loaned him some of my old books, and last week, one day, he told me that he is beginning to read the story of *The Three Musketeers*. He is taking his time to get through the book because he finds it a little difficult. He kind of likes D' Artagnan. He thinks he is so brave."

"Really now."

"Yes, he is very curious. Oh, Dad, look how he can draw those wild horses." She pulled out a piece of paper and handed it to her father. "He said this horse belongs to D' Artagnan."

"Mmm, very clever."

"He's smart Dad. Oh Dad, can he come over sometimes so you

can teach him to read better and even do some arithmetic. He wants to go to school really bad, but they say he is slow—like stupid. I think he is a smart boy. He just needs one more chance. If Miss Hope keeps him out of school she not giving him a chance to learn."

Her pleadings were very compelling and presented a case that made her dad look at her with amazement. He was stunned at the way she concerned herself with what seemed to be Roderick's circumstances—a private matter for his family. Part of Mr. Goodman knew that Roderick should be helped but the other part of him believed that he should exercise prudence when it comes to other people's family affairs.

"You have been lending him your books? That was very thoughtful. But did you stop to think that perhaps his aunt may not be able to spare him time out of his day for reading. He has to work in the shop. We will have to respectfully ask her permission."

"We Dad? No. She won't listen to me. I am only a child. In fact, I don't think she likes me. Please?"

"I am sure she likes you. All right, if you insist. Let me give it some more thought. But I can't make you any promises, his auntie has to agree."

The girl hugged her dad, thanked him, and skipped to her bedroom. She knew that she had touched the softest spot in her dad's heart: literacy.

Every genre of music from New York City to New Orleans, dominated the airwaves, late night, on Radio Jamaica and Rediffusion. It kept Mr. Goodman's company, so it seemed, now that the nighttime laughter of his dear wife was only a memory. Mr. Goodman turned down the volume on his radio so that he could unwind within the blissfulness of non-stop music while Bob Dylan paints the music of the night: *how many times can a man turn his head; pretending he just doesn't see? The answer, my friend, is blowin' in the wind; the answer is blowin' in the wind.*

Soon, the bustling city fell asleep—giving voice to the contrapuntal whistling melody of the tree frogs. Sudden rapid strobes of luminous ribbon lightning gyrated wildly in the cloudy skies—filling the house with light. A rumbling sound of thunder quickened the night air. A brief and gentle rain escorted a fresh night breeze. Across the hall in her cozy room, Chloe squinted her eyes from the splendor of the heavens and slid beneath the comfort of her covers. The Goodmans rested.

"When tomorrow evening come, a go get on one of dem big Kingston JOS bus and go far, far, away from this rotten place—to a big open shiny sea. Then, a can take off them old clothes and take me a good long sea bath. After that, a will wait for the fisherman dem boat to come up, so a can go out to sea and dive for Grouper, Snapper, and gather sea moss. When we come back to the seaside, me and the fisherman dem wi make a big fire and roast plenty fish. A wi live on the boat and never come back. Aunt Hope and dem will never find me." The tears flowed down his soft freckled face and tasted like wicked unadulterated pigs-tail brine.

From the moment these thoughts entered his psyche they would absorb him—ideas that brought on such feelings of nostalgia. Finally, on that fateful evening, he gathered every ounce of courage and willpower to follow through with his plan. As the sunsets' spectral palette of orange, red, magenta, and violet lent its colorful splendor to a picturesque Olympic Gardens horizon, Roderick, with broom in hand, stepped pass his Aunt Hope in dutiful fashion and headed for the sidewalk. On seeing the boy with the broom, she questioned, "Is where you going with the broom this late hour of the evening? A hope you not going to sweep out my riches out of the shop?" Many people on the island were convinced that it was bad fortune to sweep the dust out of their house or business establishment after sundown. Roderick feared that his super plan was definitely a failure now that Aunt Hope seemed to be in on it. In any case, he replied like a good steward, "No Auntie. A goin sweep off the piazza." Then he quickly hid the broom behind the wooden gate and headed down the street to the bus stop. As he waited for the bus to arrive, his heart began to race, and he could feel sweat rolling down his arms and face. A moment too late and Aunt Hope might spoil his plan that he so methodically devised.

A small crowd waited at the bus stop. Upon the arrival of the bus, the doors swung open. Roderick had no bus fare and so he crawled under the legs of unsuspecting folks, snuck pass the conductress, and took a seat in the back. As the bus headed towards downtown Kingston, he looked back with relief as Olympic Gardens became enveloped by the setting sun. Roderick got off at the last stop at the Parade square and headed for Kingston Harbour. As he walked towards the waterfront, he felt invisible, absorbed by the many stories Suraj told him about the harbor back in the wartimes.

Roderick hastened his footsteps because he could not wait to be a part of one of the largest natural harbors in the world. He wandered along the port taking in the breathtaking beauty of the ocean, the lights, and sounds of lovers chattering as they strolled along. Roderick felt at peace, and one with the natural beauty of the seaport. A full moon brought enough light that seemed to navigate a flock of white seagulls as they dived for fish. Roderick was amazed and looked at them with wonder as he never saw seagulls out at night when he was in the country parts. Their high-pitched shrilling call songs were like a fine fiddler's music to his ears. The cool night temperatures brought on by the northeasterly trade winds was comforting. After a while, Roderick lay on a restraining seawall to rest his sand-worn feet, tired body, and fell asleep. He could not have been sleeping long when he felt a jolt on his right shoulder.

On opening his eyes, he saw a red ribbon that stretched upwards along the seams of dark trousers that seemed to grow from the ground up. "This must be some Kingston Harbour duppy," was his instinctive thought. Somewhere between sleep and waking, it dawned on Roderick that a *red-seamed* policeman was hovering over him with a night stick in his hand. He jumped up and broke out in cold sweat. Roderick tried to fix a steady gaze at the man's red eyes looking down at him but he felt like a spider web of salt was veiling his eyes. "Little boy," he said in an authoritative baritone. Roderick wiped the web from his face.

"Wake up man. What you doing out here this time of night?"

"A waiting for Uncle to come in with him fishing boat," Roderick replied.

"Uncle?"

"Yes Uncle. I take the boat with him go out a sea all the time. Him coming for me."

"There is no boat scheduled in this part of the Harbour. Where do you live?"

"A don't live nowhere, sar."

"How you mean you don't live nowhere. Where is your mother?"

"She dead long time."

"Where your father?

"Mi noh quite know…a think him de far inna America."

"America!" This heightened the policeman's curiosity. "What is your name boy?"

"My name sir…me…me name Roderick, sir."

"Roderick what?"

"Roderick Brissett."

"Well Roderick Brissett, I will have to take you down to the station so we can figure out who you belong to," said the concerned policeman.

Roderick looked up at the policemen with some amount of trepidation, then he gathered the nerve to ask, "You not going to beat me, sir?"

"Why do you think I should beat you?"

"A get beaten fi everyting, sir. All a want was to do this time was to go see Uncle. A long fi see him."

"Well you can take that one out of your mind. I am going to find out where you live and have your folks come and get you."

Suddenly, Roderick's hopes of getting on a boat and going out to sea, to get a good sea bath, and catch some fish, came to a premature conclusion. Facing the wrath of Aunt Hope was never a part of his adventure. As the policeman turned Roderick in the direction of the squad car, the child looked over his slim shoulders at the vast sea that once brought him consolation and hope. Through his weary eyes he saw a boat pulling out on the other side of the harbor. "Wait!" he shouted from the depth of his restless soul. Roderick missed the boat—a boat that could possibly lead him to Uncle's boat on the other side of the island, well so his brain waves ebbed and flowed.

Shortly after he arrived at the police station, he was put in the custody of Corporal Allouishous who was on duty while the other police proceeded to make contact with Roderick's family. Corporal Allouishous gave him a cup of tea and some water crackers. Roderick thanked him and ate every bit of it, curled up in the corner on a bench, and dozed off.

About two hours later, two women approached the front counter at the police station. "May I help you ladies," the corporal inquired.

Hope with belt in hand and Lillian with a navy blue cotton knitted cardigan over her arm presented themselves to the officer with a sense of urgency. "I am here to get Roderick, I am his aunt," Hope informed.

The corporal pointed in the direction of the boy, "He is sleeping over there."

Hope stormed over to the boy, shook him vigorously. "Wake up bwoy! A going to bruk you two foot inna di ankle. You is a wicked likkle bwoy. What you trying to do...run away? You can cross Morgan's Harbour, with the Goodmans, out of your book."

"I am sure the boy can explain," Lillian suggested.

"Explain...mek him explain to this—

She lashed him three times across his back with the belt. He screamed. The policeman stood up instantly.

"Lady you can't do that here!"

Lillian grabbed the belt away from her and separated her from the boy.

"No Hopie. Take it easy. Mind you get in trouble."

"Trouble...him is so so trouble!" Hope yelled at the top of her lungs.

"Hopie...you are not wise," Lillian chided.

"A never bring you with me to tell me whether me wise or not. You always was Miss Holier-Than-Thou!"

"I don't want to argue. Find out from the child what happened. Perhaps he has a good reason."

"You not making any sense. Maybe you need to keep him and reason with him then," Hope lashed back and charged over to the front desk to complete the paperwork with the corporal.

Lillian gently held the boy by his hand as he sobbed and heaved uncontrollably. The tears soaked his face and mixed with fluids from his nose and mouth. "Hush, never mind. I am your Aunt Lillian. Take this handkerchief. Wipe your face," she whispered.

He wiped his face and took her in for a moment, still heaving in a temper. Then, a little smile forced its way to form on his lips. He finally met her. He had often wondered about her, what she looked like. "Aunt Li…Li…Lilyan."

"Yes…Aunt Lillian," she said.

He paused to stare at her some more. "You pretty just like Suraj said," he told her softly between heavy breaths.

"Thank you. Suraj told you that?"

"Yes Auntie. Him like you plenty plenty."

"You grow big eh…you eyes them still light and nice same way. You could do with a nice trim, your hair a little bushy," as she stroked his head.

Roderick didn't know how to accept much of her fussing over him. Yet he felt some amount of joy now that he finally met her.

"I haven't seen you since you were very small, sorry. Come, put on this cardigan, it is getting chilly outside."

Hope could see Roderick and Lillian from where she was standing. They seemed to have bonded rather quickly, like they smelled each other's blood. Soon, the three left in silence as they rode in the back seat of the cab to Aunt Hope's home. To Lillian, that night brought back unpleasant memories of the way she had left a little boy she was very fond of named Roderick, with his mother Mara'Belle, in Montego Bay.

The following Saturday evening, Chloe's father went next door to visit Miss Hope. Chloe stood on top of the piano so that she could peep over the fence into the kitchen area. Her dad and Miss Hope greeted each other cordially. She offered him a seat but he preferred to stand.

It appeared as if they were comfortable with discussing the matter at hand. Miss Hope and her dad talked for a long time. At first, the conversation seemed to be real serious, but then after a while they both started to laugh. To the girl, Hope seemed more ascetic, a rigid woman who shunned the appearance of any form of earthly delight. "I have never seen Miss Hope laugh before. She actually looked pretty," Chloe said in a loud whisper, covered her lips in case the wind carried away her thoughts. Miss Hope clapped her hands summoning Roderick to come and meet Mr. Goodman.

Roderick quickly ran to the standpipe and washed his dirty feet and hands. He rubbed the bottom of his right foot on the top of his left foot and rubbed the left over the right, as if to dry them. Then he ran his wet hands over his wooly hair that had not seen a barber's shear in months, and then he wiped them on his pants. The girl watched intently as her dad talked with Roderick for a while. He stroked Roderick on his head in a kind and gentle way unlike the touch to which he seemed to be growing accustomed. Roderick behaved like a real gentleman. Mr. Goodman shook his hand and Roderick gave the most beautiful smile. Although he looked a little scared at first, in no time, he looked happy. As her dad told Miss Hope and Roderick goodbye, Chloe scurried from the top of the piano, and stood looking up at a plaque that hung above the piano, which she had read so many times:

*Among the truly educated there is no discrimination*
*...Confucius: 551- 479 BC*

When her dad returned home, he told Chloe that Miss Hope had agreed to have Roderick come over on a Sunday afternoon for reading lessons as long as he made the effort to improve in his behavior and keep up with his chores. If he did not have any more temper tantrums, maybe she could spare him to go on the trip to Morgan's Harbour.

The girl was beaming with delight but puzzled about Miss Hope's allegations of Roderick's bad behavior. He seemed to be working too much instead of being a regular boy.

"Yippee!"

"Maybe his parents and Aunt Hope would agree to let him go to school next term," he supposed.

"But he doesn't have any parents, Dad."

"I am sure he does. They live far away in the country parts."

That evening after supper, in the quiet of her room, she had a very personal conversation with Longfellow hoping for a wonderful miracle for Roderick. "It's been a month since Dad talked with Miss Hope about Roderick who is doing everything he can to please her. But all he does is work, work, work…him will dead!"

"Work won't kill him. It is his attitude towards the work that will destroy him."

"You were always fair but you not sounding like that tonight. All I want is for my dad to just teach him to read."

"Patience Chloe. Patience. It has good merit."

The midday sun imposed its will on the comforts of the day. Roderick was scaling bright pink, fresh goat fish in the backyard over a white enamel basin with water. He carefully pulled the guts of the fish through the gill cover and placed the entrails on a sheet of newspaper. Then he chopped off the pectoral and anal fins with a knife that he kept sharp by rubbing the blade on a stone. After that, he baptized each one in cool fresh clean water. He took great pride in placing each clean and gutted fish in a big iron Dutch pot. Then he covered the pot with a piece of cardboard, safe from the swarm of flesh famished flies that exercised their license. It was quiet except for the occasional blue fly that buzzed loudly and slapped him around the ears. From nowhere, so it appeared, a pebble crashed into his enamel basin—pinggg! This frightened Roderick and he awkwardly pricked his thumb on the spiny dorsal fin of the fish he was scaling. He winced in agony at the pain and the sight of blood. Chloe watched him from a volcanic boulder that seemed to grow out of the earth, straight from Venezuela, against the concrete fence that divided the two homes. Roderick turned around to see her perched on top of the fence, laughing her head off, while the sweet juice from a blackie mango rolled down her arm.

"Yuh frighten mi yuh know!"

"Sorry. I just wanted to surprise you."

"It not good fi creep up pan people like that you know. You can get hurt like that."

Chloe still found it kind of funny to see his reaction. "Who going hurt me?"

"Not me. But look how yuh mek mi juk mi finger wid di fish bone," he grumbled curtly.

"I didn't make it happen. Is you not paying attention. Hush, never mind. A was just playing with you," Chloe consoled jokingly.

"Yuh play rough!" Roderick squeezed his thumb really hard to slow the flow of the blood, sucked it, and then he dried it in his shirt. He believed that his saliva had healing qualities and in no time his finger would be back to normal.

"When last you take up a book? You always seem to be working, working, working all the time. Look Nelton and Stephen out there flying kite and you round here scaling fish!"

"Don't watch that. Me used to this Chloe. When me was in the country me always have to work hard fi my madda. Plenty time mi don't get to go a school for me always have to tie out the goat dem early morning time. Nuff time me have to wash my brother and sister dem clothes down the river before me go a school. Me soh tired most a di time that me noh bother go a school. Me just stay a di river till the fisher man dem a go out and me folla dem." He fanned the flies away from his ears and went back to scaling.

Now it all started to make sense to Chloe. "You not slow then. You just don't get to go to school often enough."

"But me coulda tell you that long time," he said sarcastically. "Plenty time my madda say she don't have no money to send me go a school. What she get from Missa Cupidon for my brother and sister, can't stretch. Soh me just clean yard and run round and do things fi my madda most a de time. Is my teacher put it inna my madda head seh me cyaan learn. Me slow. Me just never get enough schooling like my brother and sister dem."

Roderick finished cleaning the nearly three dozen fish, wrapped the entrails in the newspaper, and dumped it in the rusty old Shell oil drum in which Aunt Hope burned garbage twice a week. A John Crow landed on an unyielding branch of a mango tree, intent on foraging the remains. The rambunctious cousins were approaching with their kites. Upon seeing the boys, Chloe retreated behind the fence. A cool breeze rustled the Lignum Vitae tree in its magnificent splendor. Friendly raindrops heralded light showers that soon washed the fishy smell down the drain.

# Chapter Six

# Into The Light

Roderick's quarters were warm and still. Not even a mouse stirred tonight. The perennial Oleander shrub below his window released a sweet fragrance. Down the hall, the women chatted as they made their way into Aunt Hope's living room for their monthly Ladies Aid meeting. A door slammed. The lamp flickered sending a cloud of smoke before settling again to a blue flame. Roderick lay worn-out upon his cot contemplating whether or not he should go musketeering before falling asleep.

Roderick was enjoying his new reading adventure. Six months had passed since he started private lessons with Mr. Goodman, a year and four months since he had seen a traditional school room. He would make time to read his books after his evening chores, especially when his cousins' youthful energy had more or less abated. He would take out the *Three Musketeers* and read quietly to himself. Some words really baffled him, but once he got over the initial awkwardness of asking Mr. Goodman to identify some of the words, reading became the center of his universe. He would go on adventures with D'Artagnan and converse with him on his every move. Even though D'Artagnan was a country boy like Roderick, he decided that D'Artagnan was the real hero in his story. At times, he found D'Artagnan a little too hotheaded but praised his courage. D'Artagnan could fight his way out of any situation, so it seemed, but Roderick was beginning to feel that there were no victories for him to win in Kingston. Yet, he was as obstinate as a mule and would not back away from fights knowing a double-beating was guaranteed recompense.

Roderick was missing the simplicity of the countryside as he looked out at the stars that became distorted by the broken windowpanes. The moon appeared to have more stars in its celestial company like feral horses riding circles around its oval mass of light. Suraj once told him that his grandmother used to tell him many stories about the way the constellation clustering of the stars formed shapes of animals during certain seasons. Punjab culture, the Land of the Five Rivers, had many myths, and as a child, Suraj found the stories fascinating. He learned to take care of the animals especially since they were often celebrated as heroes in his grandma's bedtime stories. So, too, Roderick had been caring for animals, birds, and chickens ever since he was growing up in the country.

Tonight, the horses' deafening sounds seemed to bring on a headache so fierce that Roderick felt the world closing in on his story. Out of the darkened skies, D'Artagnan appeared on an albino horse that had a deep brown tattoo around its right eye. As the hero approached, he noticed that he was wearing raggedy old clothes, he was barefoot, and carried no sword. Roderick was startled and awestruck. "There are more victories to be won…much more than you think," the loud voice of the hero penetrated the night sky like thunder rolling. Roderick was astounded at the sight. He did not know if he should be scared or embrace the hero. He called out to D'Artagnan, "Weh yuh shoes?

The hero grinned exposing his bright gold-capped incisors in his upper maxilla. "Shoes restrict the traction I need for these potholes."

Roderick tried to make sense of the hero and shot back, "Look pan yuh clothes!"

"Ah, young hero. Clothes do not make a man out of you. It is how you wear your dignity inside your clothes that matters."

Roderick's head was pounding more viciously as he writhed from one end of his cot to the other.

"Young hero...me...a hero?"

"Yes, you a hero!"

"Weh yuh sword...how yuh protect yuhself?"

"Ah! You don't need a sword. You must fight for what is right, never with the sword!"

"Oh D'Artagnan, fight? Fight is my middle name and fighting get me inna plenty worries, it noh mek fren."

"Young hero, on the contrary, fighting does make friends."

"A have two fren—Chloe and Maas Suraj. We doh fight."

"How soon you forget. Remember your first encounter with the girl. You both had a fight. Ever so slightly, you did fight with Maas Suraj. But love has since swapped places with those fights."

Roderick marveled at the wisdom of his hotheaded hero. "My cousin Nelton pick fight with me all the time."

"Next time he picks a fight with you, just listen to his actions. They are trying to teach you something about yourself. Something you need for your life's journey. I must go now." Thrice did the stallion neigh. With that, D'Artagnan rode off bravely into the night.

Roderick, overcome with fright, screamed, "D'ar...k...night!" He jumped up out of his catnap with the story book across his chest. Through the haze of sleepiness and headache he saw Nelton standing over him.

"Yuh did a dream man!" Nelton mocked. Roderick did not respond but wiped the sweat from his forehead in the cuff of his pajamas. He wandered how long Nelton may have been standing there, and if he could have been in on his tête-à-tête with D'Artagnan.

The moon vanished behind the clouds, taking the iridescent glow of the stars with it. The night wind made the frail windowpanes crackle. A peenie wallie blinked at the boy. Roderick turned his back on Nelton, with not a word, closed the book, and curled up to sleep.

The next day, Roderick welcomed the day with renewed energy. A gentle wind blew the rubbish and the leaves softly along the dirt path that led to the front of the shop. The sun crawled between the Almond and the Julie mango trees casting a silhouette of humanlike form on Olympic Way. Chi-chi birds chirped in contrasting songs to the tooting horns of buses, cars, and the peanut vendor's noisy unrelenting steam cart whistle that was now sending round puffs of moist clouds into the air.  School children played dandy shandy on the sidewalk while a lonely billy goat crossed the busy street, unaware of any danger the streets portend.

Chloe walked with poise into the shop to buy her grater cake, which Roderick had already wrapped neatly in brown paper, anticipating her arrival. He handed her the bag and said, "You don't have to pay me."

"You crazy. Your auntie will break your ribs for giving away her things."

"No, this is my gift to you. A help her to make them this time so a could get it for you."

"Thank you. But you didn't have to."

"No problem!"

Chloe knew that Roderick was elated to see her but his auntie was home early so they couldn't talk much. Roderick complained to Chloe about his cousins who were becoming ever so unbearable. "A can't stand the bwoy dem Chloe."

She firmly chided, "Is not the the bwoy dem…what you must say Roderick?"

"Awright…awright…sssh…ssssssh…a know what to say…is the boys…not the boy them!"

"Yes…that's right. The boys. One boy. Two boys. Three boys. Got it?"

"Got it!" His eyes sparkled with a measure of success and pride. The children continued to work on their grammar unaware that Aunt Hope entered the shop. She promptly broke up the session and sternly scolded, "Boy, the devil find work for idle hands." Then she turned to the girl in a sinister way, "Little gal, idle behind bring bastard." The children had no clue what she was talking about. Roderick was even more convinced that the people in Kingston just have funny ways of letting off steam in order to get their point across. As for the girl, she thought, "What on earth was Miss Hope talking about? I did not know that reading was idle."

So that afternoon, having come face to face with the wrath of a scolding from Miss Hope, Chloe paid for her sweetie, real fast, and made a hasty retreat. That evening, she wondered why such a bright boy like Roderick did not get the same kind of schooling as Miss Hope's sons. "He was learning so fast," she believed.

Spare time was hardly available to Roderick but he always found a way. He was driven by the need to show Chloe how much he was grasping and building on the lessons from her dad. Roderick sat under the cool shade of the tamarind tree and began to make corrections to the first poem he wrote for Chloe. *Thare was one pore boy* became *There was a poor boy*. *Dem take for one toy* became *They treat him like a toy*. "A tink mi get it now! A tink mi get it!" he guffawed at a long legged rooster that lifted its tail, and flaunted its shimmering red, blue and green variegated feathers. The fowl raised its majestic scarlet comb as if to acknowledge the boys happiness and simply hopped away.

Roderick was not only learning to spell words like *there* and *poor* but he was making baby-steps with nouns and articles, well that's what Mr. Goodman told him two Sundays prior. He had learned to pronounce difficult words, used past tense, and replaced the word "one" with the indefinite article "a." Roderick was learning the basic parts of speech and the way words are classified. His day to day language patterns required him to use lots of pronouns or substitutes for nouns. He quickly learned how to use the right pronouns for the right situation like "him" and "her." Although he hadn't found a word, that he liked, to rhyme with Chloe, he found great joy when he could spell her name right for the first time.

The lights were turning on in his mind and he was beginning to have fun with words. His intellect was being stimulated, his sense of reasoning, and his ability to think became more apparent, especially to Mr. Goodman. Roderick started to feel that one day he would write so well that Chloe and others would be able to understand what he was saying. Roderick reflected upon a discussion he had with Mr. Goodman during one of his lessons.

"I have absolutely no intention of taking away the normal ebb and flow of the language you are accustomed to speaking," Goodman assured him.

"What you mean by ebb and flow?"

"It is the fluid and rhythmic way you naturally speak—in and out—up and down."

"Oh, the singy songy way me talk."

"Yes. I prefer to work with your stories, especially those you are passionate about, like your poem," Mr. Goodman shared. The skillful teacher was helping Roderick to understand how important it was for him to write and read Standard English, well enough, to communicate effectively.

The more time Roderick spent on reading and writing, the less time he had in his day to quarrel or physically challenge his cousins.

Reading brought him a lot of pleasure and his temper tantrums seemed less central to his everyday survival. All indications were that Roderick might yet go to school. Miss Hope would have to find a school suitable for a boy like him. After all, he had not been in school for more than a year and he was still reading below his grade level.

Miss Hope was not optimistic about his ability to take on the demands of a city school. Mr. Goodman, on the other hand, was confident that Roderick was ready for school. He believed that it was the right of every child on the island to be in school. As for Chloe, she counted the days as she continued to hold council with her friend, Longfellow.

In the meantime, Mr. Goodman called on his colleague, Mr. Eldemire who was the principal of the Perennial All Age School where his daughter attended. He told him everything about his work with Roderick and asked him if he would accept him as a student. Mr. Eldemire welcomed the idea and suggested that he escort Roderick to register at the school. To Roderick, it seemed like eternity had passed since he had set his eyes on a school.

Sunday morning around 10 o'clock, there was something peculiar about the air. The song birds dominated the skies in large numbers, defied gravity as they glided against the cool winds that blew over their wings. The sanctimonious were fully represented from every religion firmly held on the island. They stepped with a sense of purpose, every which way through Olympic Gardens. Rabid rival dogs sniffed each other uncontested. The sunlight imbued the dark earth with raw energy that brought the best out of every tree, and fortified plants with brilliant colors.

Roderick was sweeping the sidewalk in front of the shop as if his very life depended on it. He enjoyed this part of the job because he got a chance to be outdoors and play number games with license plates on trucks, cars, busses, and even motorcycles that whisked by. Roderick loved to listen to the carefree laughter of the women.

Moments later, Roderick could hear the sound of drums and chanting that grew louder as the crowd drew closer to the shop. In the distance, he could see a crowd of women, men, and children marching along Olympic Way. He became mesmerized by the rhythmic dissonance of the drums that played counterpoint to the now rapid beat of his heart. "What's goin on?" he thought. The mid-morning sun was blinding, and emitted a striking glare that rose from the asphalt like a banshee, a messenger from the otherworld, making her ascent. The women were dressed in brightly-colored dresses and fancy head wraps, some of which seemed to touch the sky. The men wore dark pants and brightly-colored shirts, while some wrapped their heads and wore a colorful band around their waists. As the crowd got closer, Roderick could feel himself being pulled in by the hypnotic power of the drums.

His curiosity got the better of him and so he crossed the street in order to get closer to the action. Leading the band, a sect known as revivalists, was a woman as tall as a Papaw tree. The locals addressed her as Madda Bogle, another way of saying *Mother* or *Warner Woman*, one who forewarns the people of looming peril. Many viewed her as a clairvoyant, able to connect with the supernatural world. Others believed that she was that balm in Gilead, unguent for their weary feet. Madda Bogle's skin was smooth and black as the bark of an Indian Ebony tree. She wore a red dress with a green and gold ruffled sash around her waist. A pair of scissors hung from her waist band. Bright red, green, and gold fabric adorned her head, forming a huge knot above her forehead. A yellow pencil was stuck securely behind her right ear. Her neck was adorned with strings of brown, white, and red John Crow beads. Lore has it that these beads have mystical healing powers. Heaven knows there were many in need of healing today. She carried a white handkerchief in her hand, which she waved as she danced in the sunshine. The followers believed it held special powers to guard and ward off evil just like the big ring she wore on her right hand. Her countenance was uncompromising. Suddenly, she commanded the band of people to stop marching and face the direction of the shop; but the drumming and chanting continued:

*Mother the great stone got to move*
*Mother the great stone got to move*
*Mother the great stone*
*Oh the stone of Babylon*
*Mother the great stone got to move.*

The Madda's voice rose above the music and breathed out a warning, "Beware! Beware! Beware! Depart from evil and do good. Change from your wicked ways! For the wicked will surely perish!" She said this three times in their hearing.

By then, a small group of people started to gather outside the shop, curious to hear and see Madda and her band. Aunt Hope did not budge because she shared no part or lot with this sect. Some folks whispered while others laughed at the sights and sounds. However, Madda did not rest at that spot for long. In military-style drill she gave a certain signal with the scarf, the band of people made an about-turn, and they resumed the march. Roderick had gotten so close to the goings-on that he became swept up in the middle of the band. He tried to get out but the band just kept moving swiftly along the road, singing and drumming.

"Beg yuh pass…excuse me," Roderick begged almost inaudibly as he pressed against the sweaty soul-on-fire ecstatic revelers. The more he pressed, the more he got pushed toward the center of the crowd. He was levitating above the ground, defying gravity. It was as if the drums claimed him. "Is what dis Lord?" Roderick shouted. "Is what dis mi get into? Mi dead now!" No one heard his plea.

He looked around him and there were sick people, with a seriousness of purpose, hobbling along with walking sticks, and old men were moaning in pain. Women held babies who appeared to be taking their last breath. Roderick could smell the sweet fragrances that clashed with rancid odors from rub-up healing herbs. Today, the sick, lame, weak, poor, rich, educated, politician, illiterate, expatriate, young, and old, all came looking for answers to their life's angst on Resurrection Sunday. Madda was in charge. Then he felt a sudden pull and he was turned anti-clockwise and forced to face the direction of the crowd. He was walking backwards to keep up. Then a sudden fear came over him. He could hear his heart pounding in his chest as the sweat rolled down his face like a river. Without warning, the street became dark as a thick cloud masked the sun. At the strange sight, the people wailed exultantly as the drummers beat more quickening rhythms. It was as if the mighty guardian spirit of the air had stretched its hand over them. The Madda spun anti-clockwise in a circle and waived her white scarf in the air and Roderick became one with the throng.

They soon came to a yard with a large black mango tree that hung over the fence. The tree was laden with ripe fruits. About twelve feet behind the gate stood a small white-washed concrete house with a slanted zinc roof. Prominently displayed across the door was a sign that read: Gates of Zion. A red flag hung from a sash cord outside the front window. The crowd filed expectantly into the house that was set up much like a place of worship. Roderick finally could breathe.

"Excuse…excuse…excuse me please!" he pleaded with a little old lady that had stubbornly blocked his path. "A say excuse me." She hissed her teeth and he pinched her, so much so, that she slapped him with her handbag, landing him right into a seat on a bench in the left aisle. Roderick gazed in amazement at the table that was set next to the altar. It was draped with a lily-white cloth with beautiful white silk embroidery patterns sewn delicately into it. On top of the table were three lighted white candles, fresh fruits, a bowl of water, cakes, and bread. In the center of the floor was an aluminum wash pan, like a pool, filled with water.

Madda stood ceremoniously at the head of the table and started to chant a prayer that sounded much like the Catholic priest, orating a Latin liturgy that rolled off the tongue; an unknown language. Then she called on the spirits of power and light to illuminate the dark places. "Holy Ones! Holy Ones! Holy Ones! Welcome! Blessed Holy Ones! Welcome! Martha! Welcome! Thaddeus! Welcome! Hear us! Hear us! Hear us!" The people looked at her with awe as if she was the mother of all mothers under whose wings one broods—awaiting her advice. This fascinated Roderick but somehow the Madda's aura brought on some trepidation. He felt his head starting to swell and chills ran through his body. It appeared as though everywhere he looked her eyes followed him. It was as if her spirit possessed him. This scared Roderick. "Mi haf to get out a here now!" he thought as he fidgeted in his seat. Soon her prayer morphed into singing and the women dressed in white picked up a refrain.

*Don't you trouble Zion*
*Don't you trouble Zion*
*Zion have a key*
*To open sinners hearts*
*Don't you trouble Zion!*

Then the drums started to beat a hypnotic, almost dissonant sound, *boomboom boomboom boomboom breketeke boomboom*

*boomboom boomboom boomboom brekete du-dum, du-dum, du-dum* as the women and men with turbans started dancing and groaning. They were blowing deep long breaths between monotone phrases of *hema, hema, hema, hema* while Madda's high pitched, squeaky mezzo tone suddenly changed into the thunderous voice of a man as she wailed scripture verses, mostly from the Psalms, in a call and response to their groans, melodies, and the sound of the drums:

> *Fret not thyself because of evil doers; neither be thou envious against the workers of iniquity; for they shall soon be cut down like the grass and wither as the green herb. Cease from anger and forsake wrath. The wicked shall fall upon their own sword…it shall enter into their own heart.*

The people screamed and wailed at her teaching that soared high on prophetic wings and spoke directly to their circumstances. It is believed that many of the ills the people suffer on the island are a direct result of the minds of wicked and jealous people, many of whom profess to practice the craft of Obeah, or science as some people call it. Many swear by its power to destroy evil doers and others believe in its transforming powers. So, if Obeah struck the household, Madda Bogle had the cure.

The more they sang and groaned, danced and pranced, the more they became spellbound by the spirits they invited to the session. Madda waved her scarf over the pool and said a blessing. Then she invited the mothers with small children and those unaccompanied children to be the first to step in the pool of holy water. After which, she raised the chorus, which they sang over and over again. To Roderick, it seemed as if they sang for hours:

> *The water is troubled my friend*
> *Step right in*
> *The mighty power*

*Moving this hour*
*No longer stand*
*There on dry land*
*The water is troubled my friend*
*Step right in.*

As she dipped the crying children in the pool the people raised
their voices in song:

*Dip dem dip dem*
*Dip dem in the healing stream*
*Dip dem Madda Madda Dip Dem*
*Dip dem fi cure bad feelings.*

Roderick saw this as his opportunity to turn right around and
dash straight for the exit. As he positioned himself to scurry out of the
churchyard, his two eyes and Madda's two eyes locked—making four.
He froze. She continued to exhort from Isaiah 49 verse 15:

*Can a woman forget her sucking child,*
*That she should not have compassion on the son of her womb?*
*Yea, she may forget, yet will I not forget thee*
*Yea, she may forget, yet will I not forget thee.*

It was as if she spoke directly to Roderick and he felt enveloped by
a warm feeling as her eyes penetrated his very being. Roderick started
to walk backwards, in the direction of the exit, all the while, keeping
a steady gaze on Madda who chanted an entreaty:

*Bright soul*
*Wha mek yuh tun back?*
*Bright soul*
*Wha mek yuh tun back?*
*Bright soul*
*Wha mek yuh tun back?*
*Yuh ketch a river Jordan*
*An yuh tun back!*

Her chant hypnotized Roderick and he could feel his feet slowing but he knew he had to get out fast. Something was pulling him to stay and something was pulling him to leave. The latter overcame him and he ran home at lightning speed.

Hope hardly noticed that Roderick was not around, well so it appeared, as her focus shifted to her children. Nelton and Stephen were playing dandy shandy with two of the girls from the neighborhood. Roderick walked passed the children and headed straight through the open gate towards the backyard. He took a deep breath, threw his head back from apparent exhaustion. Then, he turned on the water at the standpipe, washed his face, hands, and feet.

Roderick could not wait for Chloe to return from Sunday school so that he could tell her of his chance adventure. As soon as her Aunt Frances dropped her off at the gate, Roderick ran to meet her. As if still out of breath he recounted his odyssey. "Chloe, Chloe, Chloe, you know the Revival Church down the road?"

"You mean the Poco church—yes. A pass there a few times. They make plenty noise," Chloe shared.

"Well, you not goin believe what happen today."

"Tell me…tell me!"

"A whole heap a people with drum and tambarine march pass here dis mornin."

"And what happened?"

"A follow dem go to the churchyard. A si di Madda woman wid her head wrap and she a wheel an turn. A say, Chloe…mi head start fi grow big inna di church."

"What! …Yuh went inside?"

"Yes."

"You never fraid?"

"How yuh mean? A fraid so tel a nearly pee pee up miself."

"How come your auntie make you leave the shop?"

"She was too busy to miss me. Auntie not interested in dem kind a thing. Her fren dem was inna de shop a talk whole mornin."

"You know, I heard about this but a never ever got to see them. I was always at Sunday school. I remember when my mother was very sick, she told me that every Resurrection Sunday, people would come from all over the world to get blessings from the Madda."

"True?"

"Yes. And how they give her plenty money to tell them what would happen to them. She even heals sick people. Madda rich."

"A did see a whole heap a sick people fi true. Some wid sore foot with fly a follow them and baby wid big belly and thing. All some rich lookin man wid big ring and thing a look something!"

"My mother often wished she had the courage to go see the Madda so she could heal her. But she never made it."

"Oh Chloe. The Madda have a big heart fi carry all the people dem troubles. You should see how she dip the children dem inna de pool a healing water like she a bathe dem."

"That is what good mothers do. They care for their children," Chloe plainly replied.

"Not my mother, Chloe. She couldn't care if I dead or live."

"Don't say that."

"Is di truth. Is like she forget bout me. One time when a look inna de Madda eye she say something like—

"Like what?"

Roderick tapped the side of his right temple as if to summon his brain to recall, "A remember now…she open her eye wide wide wide… beat her chest three times and say…I won't forget you."

"She talk to you personal?"

"Yes."

"Then you going to see her again?"

"Yes, a could see like she did want mi to stay wid her. But mi did fraid a her."

"I would be afraid too," Chloe concurred.

"But look all dem people weh the Madda sen come call. Dem happy so till…like dem glad fi si her. My mother nah mek no time fi si me. She hate me just like her sister Hope."

"Don't say that Roderick. I know your Aunt Hope is rough, and your mother might well be missing you."

"I don't miss her anymore," he replied acrimoniously.

"I miss my mother, Roderick."

"Your mother did love you. She did just too sick to live and love you noh more."

"Don't remind me," she said all choked up.

"Roderick Brissett!" His aunt yelled from the shop window. The children sensed trouble. "A have to run inside now. We talk tomorrow," he hoped.

"Promise?"

"Promise!" he affirmed.  The children interlocked their pinky fingers on their right hand in a pledge of allegiance and went their separate ways.

The summer months went by quickly and Roderick was beginning to feel that reading kept him out of trouble. His Aunt Hope did not seem to mind freeing him up on Sunday afternoons to take lessons with Mr. Goodman. Roderick wished that his mother would write to him so he could read her letters. "Maybe she forgot to give it to Missa Cupidon to put in the postbox," he sometimes wondered. Roderick reminisced about the look on his auntie's face when he thanked her for giving him time to read. "My Aunt Hope smile for real real real." Although at times she made him feel that he was ungrateful, deep in his heart he knew he was thankful for good things.

The summer of 1968, opened the gates to faraway lands, peoples, and cultures. Mr. Goodman didn't teach him to read only, he taught him about life outside of the island of Jamaica. Roderick learned that young children were just like him in other parts of the world. Some students protested against oppression and injustice, they wanted equal rights. The school room was often a place where fights broke out. He learned of great men who were martyred for what they believed was right. Roderick felt lucky to be alive and to have someone like Mr. Goodman in his life.

Roderick finished washing down the shop floor and then he ironed Nelton and Stephen's school uniforms. He handed the clothes to Stephen who stood patiently in the doorway, took the clothes and thanked him. Nelton peeked over Stephen's shoulders and sniggered as Roderick walked towards his quarters.

"You can say something yuh know Mister Man," ragged Nelton.

Roderick paused, looked the boy up and down, "What yuh want mi fi say?"

"You can ask me how me do."

"I don't want to know how yuh do…is none a my business," Roderick lashed a quick retort.

"You don't want to talk to me, Mister Man?"

"You is so so trouble yah…Suraj always tell me trouble don't set like Kingston rain."

"Suraj, Suraj…is all you talk bout…so what bout we…we not somebody too?"

"Is my fren that…him nice to me," he mumbled and walked away.

Roderick sat at the edge of his cot contemplating the happenings of the day. Then it suddenly dawned on him, the parting words of D'Artagnan, "Next time he picks a fight with you…just listen to his actions. They are trying to teach you something."

"Maybe Nelton want me fren with him. Mmm. No. Mi doh think so. As if that was all a need fi get me out of this miserable shop life." Whenever Roderick could not unravel life's mysteries it made him feel a bit of disquiet. He would think of something to draw about nature.

And, so, later that evening he took out the paintbrush and drawing paper. A woman and child was his muse and inspired him to create a great gift which he hoped to give his Aunt Lillian some day. The evening was hot and still except for the men playing dominoes at the yard behind the shop. Every Sunday evening, the old Mason entertained his buddies from the Lodge. They would roast corn, salt fish, and pickled-pork. Liquor was served in abundance from over proof rum to Red Stripe beer—a brew of fine quality. The men would have spirited conversations about anything from city life, morality, and politics, interspersed with hearty guttural laughter. Roderick listened as their voices morphed with the frogs and distinctive chirping sounds of the male crickets. He imagined the freedom the men enjoyed. "It mus a so easy fi be a man. One day. One day, and the night will belong to me."

It was one year and eleven months since Roderick arrived in Olympic Gardens. Roderick got dressed to meet the school principal. He wore a white long-sleeved shirt, a pair of hand-me-down black pants from his cousin Nelton, who was just a little shorter than he was. As a result, the pants were above his ankle. He wore black shoes and white socks. Roderick did not seem to mind at all. He knew for sure that his clothes were clean and well ironed because he had done it himself. He was actually proud of his appearance. Although he could have done with a haircut, every strand of hair was patted tightly in place, and his face and neck glowed with coconut oil.

Mr. Goodman pulled up the 1958 Rambler four-door sedan in front of the shop. It was powder pink with shiny sheet metal strips and a beige hardtop roof. Roderick shyly got into the front seat and sat next to Mr. Goodman. "Good afternoon Mr. Goodman."

"Good afternoon Roderick. How is your day so far?"

"Fine sir."

"Ready for your big adventure?"

"Advencha sir?"

"Yes. Your first day to meet the principal of the school."

"Oh. That you mean," and he chuckled. "Ready, sir."

The car looked and smelled like a brand new vehicle from the showroom. The control panel on the dashboard with its lighted navigation instruments was fascinating to Roderick. He stroked and pressed down on the soft leather seats that bounced back like an air-filled balloon. He twitched from side to side, not from discomfort, but wondered if the moment was real. He had never experienced a car ride before.

The drive to Perennial All Age was only ten minutes, just before the Bay Farm Road crossing, and Roderick kept his eye on the road. The steel-tire wheels, made for rural roadways, took steadily to the Kingston streets like a hydraulic dump truck. It resisted the afternoon trade winds like a smooth airplane ride. Mr. Goodman was listening to the news on Radio Jamaica that reported protests on the campus of the University of the West Indies. To Roderick, it would appear as if all of Kingston would soon be engulfed in fire or something horrible was coming on the city. However, Mr. Goodman did not volunteer any information to shed any light on what the boy was thinking. "Almost there," informed Mr. Goodman, pointing in the direction of the school.

Roderick could see the school just ahead on a flat lay of land, nestled between some wooden houses, with lattice designed doors, and sturdy window jambs. Some of the houses were surrounded by either barbed wire, zinc or brick fences. There was a Shell gas station to the right where a barefooted boy, around twelve, in tattered pants and no shirt, sold newspapers on the outside. The Rambler stopped at a traffic light long enough for Roderick to take note of the rows of businesses that were opened for trade. Across the street from the school was the Gourzong Haberdashery. There was Lynn's Poultry Farmhouse where they sold live chickens and grain, and Blossom's Dressmaking shop. On the landing, vendors sold sweets, fruits, pencils, pens, crayons, balloons, toys and any imaginable trinket a child could desire. Children were busy examining the merchandise and posing like real big time bargain shoppers with a take it or leave it stance.

On their arrival at the school, Roderick's eyes panned his surroundings like an Oscar Micheaux movie camera, one of the first black filmmakers he discovered on one of his reading adventures. The two-story concrete L-shaped school building was painted off-white with dark-green trimmings. There was a wide playfield to the east. At the center, was a majestic Blue Mahoe tree, with sprawling branches, laden with green heart-shaped leaves, and bell-shaped yellowish-orange flowers. Humming birds danced a fluid ballet in elegant style as they fed off its sweet nectar. Under its motherly shade, children played hand-clapping games or chatted. in groups in the eighty plus degree heat. Some held hands and swung them as they skipped to catch the next bus home. The cacophony of sounds made Roderick's imagination of being a part of this reality, pleasingly consuming.

Mr. Goodman and Roderick walked along the labyrinth-like narrow corridors to the principal's office. There they were greeted warmly by Mr. Eldemire.

"Good afternoon gentlemen," he said.

"Good afternoon sir," Mr. Goodman and Roderick replied in unison.

"I am so glad you could make it."

"Thanks for having us," Mr. Goodman responded. "I suppose you have heard about the unrest at the University."

"Troubling, very troubling," Eldemire opined. "I trust that it will not escalate into uncontrollable furor."

"The police have been brought in to control the situation but nothing is certain as of the last bulletin," Mr. Goodman added. "When national pride is threatened, it is the students who rise up. What else can I say my brother."

"I guess you are right, I am glad you gentlemen could make it here anyway."

Roderick listened with intent, uncertain of the nature of the happenings except that it sounded like an awful omen. Today was no time for dreadful things to happen—it was his opportunity to get school right. For a brief moment, he drifted in thought.

"Tell me young man. How was the drive here?"

"It was fine, sir. Mr. Goodman drive good, sir." Roderick started to compose himself and dried his sweaty palms against the leg of his trousers. The next fifteen minutes were spent filling out papers with all the pertinent information the school would need to get him placed in the right class. The goodly sire then signed—*Isaac Goodman for Hope Flowers, 16 October 1968*. That marked the very day the riots spilled onto the streets of Kingston in protest of Prime Minister Hugh Lawson Shearer's edict that the Guyanese revolutionary thinker and advocate for the Caribbean's destitute poor blacks, Walter Rodney, was not welcome back on the island, he was expelled indefinitely.

Students from the University of The West Indies at Mona, in Kingston, where Rodney lectured, protested against what they considered the kind of colonial hysteria that perpetuated the ignorance and mental slavery. An edgy citizenry believed this politically motivated panic was under the sole custody of the traditionalist government. The students viewed the Prime Minister's actions as a blatant ploy to silence the voices of youthful intelligence and reason that were emerging in the early years of a post-independent Jamaica. Roderick feared that the riots might reach Olympic Gardens, too, and he became fidgety.

After reviewing the application, Mr. Eldemire turned to them and said, "This boy is welcome in our school any day. Oriens ex occidente lux, a light rising from the west." Both men shared a knowing smile— homage to the brotherhood. Mr. Goodman turned to Roderick, "Say thank you."

"Thank you, sir."

"A very polite boy indeed." Mr. Goodman was delighted and thanked Mr. Eldemire. He assured him that he would see to it that Roderick attended regularly and completed his homework. "I wish more parents were like you."

"Oh by the way, I apologize for his Aunt Hope's absence. She had to stay behind because she had no help in the shop. She asked me to convey that she could not spare him for a few more months, he is her only helper, and the busy season is fast approaching."

"No problem at all." Then he turned to Roderick and said, "I am sure you will be a fine young man some day. I look forward to seeing you next term. The holidays are just around the corner—so enjoy the rest of the time with your family."

"Yes, thank you sir," Roderick replied. And so, that night, in the soft glow of the *Home Sweet Home* kerosene lamp that attracted a multitude of brown moths, Roderick wrote a letter to his mother.

*Dear Mama,*

*A cant come to why you jus up and sen me away. I miss everybody bad bad bad. A hope you and Missa Cupidon and my brother and sister them are well. Me and auntie and Stephen and Nelton are fine. I am trying to get along with my cousin them but I like the bigger one better than the likkle one. Aunt Hope promas to let me go to this new school not far from the shop if I do my shop work. I miss country a hole heap. I make a new fren. She name Chloe Goodman. She very pretty. Her eye them so bright. She live with her father next door to the shop. Her father help me a hole heap with my reading my writing and my sums. Chloe up to even len me her book them to read a night time. If a dont get on aunt Hope last nerves she say she will make me go to Port Royal with Chloe them.*

*It hot hot hot a town. A spend most a the day in the shop. Kingston people awright but them ask too much question. I forget to tell you. I have another fren. A old Indian man. He name Mr. Suraj. Him so jokify. He come into the shop every day and buy a flaks of Bay Rum and drink it down. Mama him don't even get drunk. Sometime I feel so sorry for him. Mose of him family dead. Aunt Lillian plan to come see me when she get a chance. I trus if all go well I can come back to the country side some day. Say hello to every body for me.*

*Your son,*
*Roderick*

With that, he sealed the letter in an old, brown, government envelope he had found in the shop, and then he put it in his grip. Perhaps, one day, he will see his mother again so that he could read it to her. He blew out the lamp light. The moths vanished.

*Chapter Seven*

# Grand Market

Christmas was coming· and Roderick wanted desperately to experience the wonders of a big city holiday. He was showing no signs of slowing down as a reader and his drawings seemed to calm him down a bit and kept him out of trouble. He had worked very hard to live up to his Aunt Hope's expectations, especially, since the autumn months came around and Kingston seemed to flaunt its festivities like no other city on the island. Although Roderick had missed out on going to Morgan's Harbour with Chloe and her dad, Miss Hope promised to reward him for good deportment by sending him to Grand Market with his Aunt Lillian. This magnificent, colorful, noisy, and celebratory marketplace was at the center of the Christmas reveling. Bright red and white Poinsettias bloomed in clay pots on window sills, inside people's homes, and along the sidewalks of business places. Star lights and firecrackers lit the autumn skies as traditional carols piped through speeding cars, and from transistor radios tied to the back of bicycles that competed with sound systems in bars. If you were lucky, you got to see the Jonkonnu masquerade dancers, dressed in their flamboyant costumes; do pantomime through the streets to the sound of drums, fifes, and multi-holed, sharp, spiky aluminum graters they scraped with a stick to make music. Some of their costumes mimicked the aristocracy of their former European colonizers. Children and adults found great joy in characters like the King and Queen, Cow Head, Horse Head, Pitchy-Patchy, Belly Woman, and the petulant Policeman. It was a kind of unscripted Commedia dell' Arte of sixteenth century Italy. Theirs too is a comic showcase that pokes fun at society.

All day, Roderick's anxiety made him feel like he was in a Ferris wheel. His thoughts of what the trip would portend kept him suspended between the highs and lows of giggles and uncertainty. He aspired to look the finest he had ever looked, even in his cousin's hand-me-downs. Nelton had struck again! To Roderick, Nelton was the likely culprit who took the only pair of socks that he had washed and hung with his merino on the line to dry. Roderick knew that if he did not compose himself during this mysterious disappearance of the socks, Grand Market would only be in his imagination. And so, he set out to find his socks in the boy's room. As he searched, he sang in Nelton's hearing, a little song Uncle taught him three Christmases ago when they were painting the shed of the old community church in Browns Town. It was a parody of the popular Christmas carol, "While Shepherds Watched Their Flocks by Night."

*While shepherds wash dem socks one night*
*And heng dem pan de line*
*Some dutty tief was passin by*
*And say dem socks a mine!*

Nelton bellowed, "A who you a call tief?"

"Mi noh call noh name…if a yuh tief mi socks… yuh tief mi socks!" Roderick lashed back, although he did so almost inaudibly between closed teeth.

"The two of you stop it right now," reprimanded Stephen. "This is neither the time nor the season for all this quarrelling."

"Stephen…dis boy need to just gimme mi socks…mi nah ramp wid him today!"

"Give him his socks if you have it Nelton."

"Him need to say him sorry fi call mi tief first."

"If is me yuh a wait fi say sorry…yuh can nyaam di socks…yuh look hungry anyway!" This whole scenario rubbed Roderick the wrong way but he was not about to let Nelton get in the way of his happiness. Roderick paused, took a deep breath, listened to Nelton's actions, and walked away singing his little song:

*Mi do believe, Mi mus believe*

*Dat chink it betta dan flea*

"You ole heathen you!" Nelton yelled out at Roderick. But Roderick continued to sing, intent on keeping his composure, yet poking fun at Nelton:

*For pan di wall dem play football*

*Widout a referee…*

Roderick was just too tired of Nelton's nonsense and he was not about to fight today. Yet, he could not resist the opportunity to clench his fist, hold it up to his own mouth, make three hundred and sixty degree circles, and make a funny-faced grimace at Nelton, a kind of non-verbal victory. This was Roderick's way of saying to the boy, "I will punch you in your mouth." At that moment, he had reconciled within himself that he would be better off without the socks that day. Then it was time to get dressed to meet his Aunt Lillian. Roderick wore his white striped short sleeved shirt and his navy blue short pants. He sported his only pair of shoes, which he always kept clean and shiny. Whenever they were not being worn, he stuffed the toes with newspaper to maintain the shape.

Roderick carefully picked up the artwork that he had worked on for several weeks as a present for his Aunt Lillian. It was his rendition of a beautiful woman holding her baby boy snug in her arms, sitting sidesaddle on a shiny chestnut-colored mustang horse, escorted by D'Artagnan on foot. The woman's countenance was fire bronze and her head was crowned with a bright gold and green turban. She was dressed in a long, white, Indian cotton dress with embroidered collars. Her neckline was adorned with red and black spotted John Crow beads strung into a necklace; a cultured showpiece of elegance. She wore coconut shell earrings with a white barble dove on a tree branch delicately etched on its surface. This elegant lady was barefooted. Her baby boy, around three years, was dressed in a khaki colored pants and no shirt. He, too, was barefooted. Their faces were illuminated by a bright yellow sun and floating clouds that seemed to veil the Blue Mountains. "I hope she likes it," he whispered as he held it carefully against his chest.

Then there was a rapping on the gate. "Hoo hooooo!" Aunt Hope called out.

"Hoo hooooo! Is me Lillian."

"Come on in!" She swung the wooden gate open and hugged her sister with a warm embrace. They were happy to see each other by the way they took turns to spin each other for a look over inspection.

Hope inquired, "How you?"

"I am fine thanks," Lillian replied.

"Hey there, Ellen. You looking very festive today," observed Hope.

"Yes, mi dear. Happy holiday! Can't wait to meet your nephew. Lillian talks about him often."

"He is inside getting dressed…but knowing him, he is ready already."

Lillian was a woman in her mid sixties who had lived with her mother all her life. She never married, and she had no children. After she graduated from primary school, she went to work in Mother Flower's Cold Supper Shop and Bar at Three-Miles. Then, on impulse, she followed her sister Mara'Belle to Montego Bay but returned shortly after because the two could not get along. She spent several years working in the bar and when her mother became ill she had to take over the business. In a few years, she became a very frugal businesswoman whose outgoing personality kept her customers coming back day after day, and year after year. Lillian helped to put her six younger siblings through school. As her mother's condition declined, Lillian asked her best friend Ellen Birch to help her out in the business. The two girls had been best of friends ever since they met one summer in the country at Ellen's grandparents. Ellen was a celebrated artist who got her early exposure to fine arts at the Jamaica School of Art in downtown Kingston. Although Lillian spent a great deal of time caring for her ailing mother, her evenings were spent in laughter, writing in her diary, and sipping tea with her best friend Ellen who painted or sculpted. They continued the tradition of community by inviting friends over, many of whom were old patrons of Mother Flowers. Fourth Friday night of every month was for drinks, good food, board games, and music from all over the world.

Roderick could hear the laughter of the women as he tried to get closer to the living room; a part of the house he was not allowed to spend time in, except on occasions like these when Miss Hope wanted to make a good impression. "Roderick!"

"Yes Auntie."

"Your aunt is here!"

"Coming Auntie," his face lit up like a stadium bulb. Roderick could not contain his joy as he charged down the hall, passed the boys' room with his present for his aunt, but he would have to wait his turn. Upon hearing Aunt Hope summon Roderick, Nelton and

Stephen made a quick dash ahead of him to greet their aunt and her friend. The cousins had already taken his spotlight; well, so it seemed. In any case, he was excited that he was going to take a ride into the city on the Omnibus, a far cry from Gilford's old Sull.

"Hello Aunt Lillian and Miss—

"Miss Birch," chimed in Aunt Hope.

"Hello Miss Birch."

"How you do Roderick. Looking sharp today," Aunt Lillian observed.

"Fine Auntie. A have a present for you." He handed his aunt the painting.

"Thank you, Roderick. This is so nice of you," and she shared it with her friend. Ellen was thrilled at the way he adroitly juxtaposed his ideas and artistry to create a composition so profound. She couldn't help smiling from ear to ear. Ellen was taken aback at the details, his use of color, and the message he seemed to convey. She could hardly imagine what may have been going through the child's mind. "You did this all by yourself?" Ellen questioned.

"Yes…me do it all by myself. Me love to draw."

"I never know the boy had it in him," Aunt Hope said dumbfounded. "When you find time to do all this. Where you get the paint from?"

Roderick held his head down and did not say a word as he was not confident to express the kind of answer his Aunt Hope expected.

"You have a real artist on your hand, Hopie," Lillian said with much conviction.

"Roderick, you should come up and spend some time with me and I can show you some of my artwork," Ellen encouraged.

"If it all right with my Aunt Hope. Maybe a can make it," he responded shyly.

Hope responded snippily, "Listen noh, this boy have work to do around here!"

Lillian sensed some awkwardness, and that Ellen may have asked too much, but came back smoothly, "No problem, she will give you the time…right little sis?" she pinched Hope's cheeks.

"As long as him do him work and stop the rough- housing around here a might consider it." Lillian felt it was time to go, and so she took Roderick by the hand, and everybody said their goodbyes.

The bus traveled down Spanish Town Road into the city, dodging potholes and pedestrians who skillfully crossed the streets without looking left and right for oncoming traffic, so it appeared to the boy. Roderick sat at the window where he could take in the sights while Aunt Lillian read poetry, and Ellen crocheted. Roderick turned to his Aunt Lillian, "The people them house so broke down. I never see so much broke down place a country. All them business place perch up between people house. Our home them look much brighter in the countryside. We paint up the place when Christmas time. We red ox-dye wi veranda and white-wash the sidewalk. The people them don't seem to take care of them goat and fowl. Them just stray cross the busy road a town."

His aunt Lillian was amazed at the way he articulated his observation. "Oh Roderick, this is not the way all of Kingston looks. We have fine homes that people take great care of—

"Look Auntie" Roderick pointed in the direction of his interest. "Is the burying ground!"

Aunt Lillian quickly grabbed and lowered his pointed finger. She believed that pointing fingers at the resting place of the dead can attract a bad omen. Stories have been told of persons whose fingers rotted and fell off because the dead were disturbed. "That's May Pen Cemetery. It has a lot of history my dear. Great men and women who fought in the war are buried there. My father was laid to rest there, having died in the great train wreck at Kendal in 1957."

"Sorry about your father, Auntie—

"He is also your grandfather!"

"My grandfather…I never see a picture of him before."

"There is a picture of him on the record changer in Aunt Hope's living room."

"Mi don't go in there pan purpose."

"Really?"

"Yes. Only when mi sweep di floor. It dark like what."

"Is that right?"

"But Auntie, how come the burying ground so bushy bushy?"

"Constant rain this past season makes the place fertile and green. Church folks volunteer ever so often to clean it up. When we go by to lay flowers at Daddy's grave, we chop away the weeds around his headstone. Anyway, Christmas is a time to celebrate life!"

Half an hour later, the over-crowded bus pulled into the station on King Street, and Lillian, Ellen, and Roderick disembarked, and walked towards the central hub of the happenings. Roderick felt dwarfed as he looked up in wonderment at the tall buildings, bright lights in the show windows, vendors selling toys for little girls and boys, a bona fide Santa Claus who sat outside the Parade Store, surrounded by screaming children. The sound of Christmas carols chimed through jukeboxes in almost every store. The Rara Store was Ellen's favorite because she looked forward to great bargains every year. Just as they got to the door, Festus the clownish poppy-show greeted them. He is a famous store crier, a young man, nicely tailored with low cut hair, and about twenty-five years old. He gestured to them with a smile as he sang his commercial tune.

*Step into the Rara Store*
*The Rara Store*
*The Rara Store*
*Where you get much more*
*Pantie—fi yuh auntie*
*Tie head—fi her dry head!*

This amused Roderick but Aunt Lillian and Miss Birch did not find it funny, they were proper ladies. Anyway, they all went inside to shop. Roderick's tactile instincts kept his inquisitive hands fingering fine shirts and sweaters. It seemed that anything he needed, he would get today as he held a sweater up to his chest.

"Try it on," Miss Ellen encouraged. "It looks just like you."

Roderick smiled and said, "Is all right miss. I just know this one will fit me good. Me don't have to try it on."

Hours later, Roderick was fully loaded up with lots of gifts. He hugged his Aunt Lillian and thanked her. Then he turned to Ellen and said, "Me can call you Auntie?" Roderick was feeling a little awkward to address an adult by her first name—that was unheard of on the island.

Ellen smiled, took Roderick by the hand, and patted him gently on the right cheek, "Yes dear, you may call me Aunt Ellen."

"Thank you too Aunt Ellen for my wonderful presents. I really like my new dress shoes and the leather sandals you buy for me."

"You are very welcome, dear."

The trio was getting hungry and so they bought snacks of coconut drops, wangla cake, and flavored aerated water drinks. Lillian suggested that they take a stroll along King Street so that she could show Roderick some places of historical value. Trees lined the sidewalks on both sides casting shadows along the black asphalted street that showed visible signs of remnants of the steel tracks from a gilded tramcar era. Buses pulled in and out with passengers going uptown. Ellen stopped by a vendor who sold art and craft. "You two go ahead, I will catch up with you in a few."

Lillian and Roderick walked a few feet further and sat on a concrete bench under a shade tree. Behind them stood the General Post Office that had been in operation for nearly two hundred years. Immediately across the street was the Supreme Court. The courthouse was an old colonial multi-level off-white building that took up some two city blocks. Romanesque columns supported the structure and made it look like a citadel, protecting the will of the people. Random large wood-framed opaque glass windows were half-opened to let in the Kingston breeze. Beautiful flower beds burst onto the sidewalk, flaunting varied shades of red, purple, pink, green, and sprinkled with clusters of yellow dandelion. Acacia trees lined the walkway and the bottom half of the trunks were white-washed. There was a lot of movement of people in an out of the building: women in nicely tailored skirts, cotton blouses and clutch bags, men in dark suits carried leather bags, children, and folks who sold fresh flowers. A policeman stood vigil in the doorway. Lillian pointed out that "An alley ran behind the building where the prisoners were escorted into the courthouse on court day."

Roderick's eyes popped wide open, "Fi real real real!"

"Yes, it is real. This keeps them from the view of tourists and people like us who just want to spend some time downtown."

"Oh."

"Many historical cases have been tried there by the judges," Lillian continued. "It is one of the highest seats of justice on the island."

"Justice?" Roderick's interest was immediately stirred. He wondered where he heard that word before. Then it dawned on him that he heard it from the old man. "Justice must be a very important word," he assumed.

"Yes justice. The court presides over cases in which a person's freedom is violated by others."

"Freedom?"

"Yes, freedom. Everybody has the right on this island to live in a safe place where they are not restricted and mistreated."

The thoughts of justice and freedom played hopscotch in his head, he didn't know in which box to process each marker. The conversation rested for a while as the duo savored every delightful burst of tropical flavor. He shared his coconut drops with the pigeons that seemed to boast quite snobbish palates.

The smell of sugar cane was intoxicating and brought back memories of the old countryside as a young man stopped nearby to sell his last few stalks of cane. Roderick stared absorbedly at the design of the cart and the ingenious way in which the steering wheel of a car was the navigating mechanism. He took in the young man who whistled and stripped each stalk with his sharp cutlass, with great precision and style. Then there was silence as thick as countryman cornmeal pone, one would need a hatchet to cut through it.

Lillian noticed that the boy had stopped eating and that his mind was in another place, another time. "Penny for your thoughts," Aunt Lillian proposed.

"My tawts. My tawts—

Vivid pictures of happier times with his mother teaching him how to peel sugarcane with his teeth, surfaced. There was so much laughter between them that day, he was remembering, like it was yesterday.

"A did just spit out the trash from the last sweet piece of red ribbon sugar cane when everyting like it bruk way. Mama was holing on to him jacket—crying. She was pushing me on him—she was begging him to take me with him. Him tell her him neva want her no more—she and her little bastad pickney. Him push her so hard she fall down pan de ground. Then, him pull way himself from her. Him walk go and sit down inna di car—him slam di door hard. A remember—is a blue fish-tail car. Another man pick up him bag and put it inna di trunk. Then, the man go round to the other side inna the road and drive off di car. The tall yellow man left mi madda pan di groun a hold me pan one shoulder, and the jacket inna the nother one. She buss out a scream—loud, loud, loud. Mi put mi hand pan mi ears them. She drop me so—boof—pan the hot ground, and walk way leff me go back up the hill. Is a long, long walk wid the sun a pelt down pan me. A follow behind her. She never look back fi see if me did a come. She couldn't stop cry. That was the day my father leff me and mi mother in the hot sun a the square. A was five year old." The tears swelled up in his eyes but they never fell down his face. He ground his teeth and looked off into space.

"Oh my, my, my. You never see smoke without fire. I always knew something was into something," his aunt gleaned from his story. Lillian held the boy gently against her chest, rubbed his head, and did not say another word.

Ellen caught up with them and Roderick continued to take in the sights and the sounds. He was amazed that in all of the hoopla, the well tailored Salvation Army lady in her military-style uniform, rang her bell and chanted, as generous passersby dropped coins in her bright red kettle, "Keep the pot boiling, boiling, boiling, keep the pot boiling, boiling, boiling." Ellen slipped a coin into his hand so that he too could experience the joy of hearing it sing a righteous carol with the other coins in the kettle. This would ensure that poor people had a meal at Christmas.

On their way back to the bus terminus, Roderick thought about his friend Suraj. "I wonder if him wife family and fren dem wi give him any present fi Christmas?" He felt so lucky. He remembered Suraj telling him that the only way he would experience true freedom was to give generously. Today, he felt a deep sense of freedom in the big city. Roderick knew how much Suraj meant to him; he had become

Roderick's true friend. Roderick had just encountered kindness he had only dreamt about. Now he felt it was his turn to buy gifts for his new friends, Chloe and Suraj. Lillian suggested that he would get the best bargains at the bazaar a few stores down.

Hurriedly, he unwrapped the coins that were tied in an old foot of sock. Roderick had been saving his pennies from the sale of his barble dove stone art. Now, this was his opportunity to get a gift for his new friends. He bought a Panama hat for Suraj to protect him from the sun. For Chloe, he got a bright red view-master with pictures of exotic cities from all over the world. Through these lenses, she could see the Taj Mahal, she could see the Eiffel Tower, and she could see Mount Kilimanjaro from the heart of Olympic Gardens. He liked the gifts, and so did Lillian and Ellen. He hoped his friends would like them too. But his gifts were like a tiny precious stone lost in the wind driven hot Sahara Desert dust, compared to the ones he got from Chloe all year long. Hers had been the gift of friendship and a glimmer of hope to get a first-class education at one of the finest primary schools in Kingston.

The sun was slowly setting between the asymmetrical contours of municipal buildings, shops, and shade trees. The mesmerizing sounds of music, chatter, and laughter seemed to welcome the tail end of a cool autumn breeze off Kingston's waterfront, which brought with it the smells of ripened exotic fruits, and the effluvia of body sweat, stagnant sidewalk gutter water, and vehicular emission of waste gasses.

The atmosphere made light hearts of friends, families, vendors, and tourists who added color and texture to downtown Kingston's holiday spirit. Roderick's face lit up like an aircraft landing strip, a testament to what must have been the happiest day of his life since he left the country on a punitive exchange.

Roderick sat still in the corner seat on the bus, pressed his tired forehead against the window while clutching his many presents in his arms. As he looked back at downtown Kingston, he could see fluffy clouds with silvery linings, pepper lights on buildings, street lamps, and starlights as they morphed in the distance to form one giant light bulb. The prattle among tired children, the laughter between strangers and friends, on the crowded bus, became one loud hum. The beauty, the bustle, and decorations of downtown Kingston now etched in his impressionable mind became a new picture for Roderick to draw and paint. Yet, it would disappear so quickly behind a more pragmatic picture that contended for center stage, and brought on a sense of angst upon his heart, his despair—prime for sublimation towards creative expression.

Roderick reflected upon the brutal treatment he had been subjected to all these years from his mother. What was more mystifying was the beatings and hard work he had to endure at the hands of Aunt Hope. He asked himself, "If mama neva want me … why she neva give me away to Aunt Lillian then…she nicer than Aunt Hope and the boys? At least Aunt Lillian mek me feel like somebody want me." A fruit fly landed on his nose, interrupting his plaintive thoughts, and he almost lost control of his prized bags. He looked over at Aunt Lillian who smiled at him, lovingly, and went back to her reading.

Then for a brief moment there was an everlastingly deafening silence inside his head. In a flash, thoughts came rushing in. "What could mek dem so vex wid mi? Nobody child fi suffer so. When I get big. When I get big." His feelings about his world ran like thoroughbreds at Caymans Race Track, with furlongs to go, and no finish line in view. They competed with distorted visions of hope for an education at Perennial and the uncertainty of staying in Olympic Gardens where he could spend time with Maas Suraj, Chloe, Mr. Goodman, Aunt Lillian, and Aunt Ellen, the most beautiful fragranced flowers hand-picked by providence.

*Wheel and Come Again*

# CHERRY GARDENS

*Continue the Journey with Roderick*

## Order Form

Telephone orders: Call 914.668.5836.

Email orders: egwechi@gmail.com

Checks or Money Orders: Egwechi Publishing, P.O. Box 2009, Mount Vernon, New York  10551.

Specify the number of copies and where to send them.

Name: _____

Address: _____

City: _____ State:_____ Zip:_____

Telephone: _____ Fax:_____

Email: _____

Additional shipping charges will apply.

Please send information on: ____ Other Books ____ Book Signings/ Seminars/Speaking Engagements.

**Order online at www.Amazon.com**

# Special Thanks

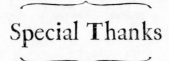

*To:*

Tamarind Festival of Caribbean Literature in Washington, DC

*For:*

2009 Lorna Goodison Caribbean Award
for Transformative Literature

http://tamarindfestival4caribbeanliterature.wordpress.com/

# About the Author

**Andrene Bonner** is an educator, writer, poet, singer, director, producer, and an accomplished actress. She was born in Kingston, Jamaica, where she attended Central Branch Primary School, Merl Grove High School, Jamaica School of Speech and Drama and the Jamaica School of Dance (now co-opted under the Edna Manley College of the Visual and Performing Arts). She holds a Master of Science in Education with Distinction, a Master of Arts in Language and Literacy, and a Bachelor of Arts in Theatre Arts and Dance with an option in Acting and Directing.

Bonner's writings have been published in *Kapu-Sens: California State University Northridge Literary Journal, Carib Press Newsmagazine, Café Africana Journal, Poets Orators Writers Artist Journal,* and will appear in the *23rd edition of The Caribbean Writer* Fall 2009. *Olympic Gardens* is the first in a trilogy and is set in Jamaica. It received the prestigious *2009 Lorna Goodison Caribbean Award for Transformative Literature* on June 14, 2009 at the *Tamarind Festival of Caribbean Literature in Washington, D.C.* Her professional affiliations include, but are not limited to, the Phi Delta Kappa Professional Association in Education (PDK), National Council of Teachers of English (NCTE), Conference on College Composition and Communication (CCCC), NAACP New York Chapter, Los Angeles Women in Music, and the Poetry Society of America (PSA). Andrene is Founder and Artistic Director of *Caribbean World Arts and Culture, Inc.*, a nonprofit organization dedicated to research, advocacy, preservation, and exhibition of works that reflect the Caribbean experience.